Blairsville Junior High School
Blairsville, Pennsylvania

MIGHTY MO

The Story of an African Elephant

My thanks to a great white hunter and conservationist, Donald Ker, who read *Mighty Mo* in manuscript and kindly gave it his blessing.

Jocelyn Arundel

Also by Jocelyn Arundel and Wesley Dennis

MIGHTY MO

The Story of an
African Elephant

by Jocelyn Arundel

Illustrated by Wesley Dennis

McGraw-Hill Book Company

NEW YORK   TORONTO   LONDON

To my mother, who would gently persuade an elephant to move if she wished to see a flower that grew beneath its foot.

Contents

"THE WILDLIFE OF TODAY IS NOT OURS TO DISPOSE OF AS WE PLEASE. WE HAVE IT IN TRUST. WE MUST ACCOUNT FOR IT TO THOSE WHO COME AFTER."
— KING GEORGE VI OF ENGLAND —

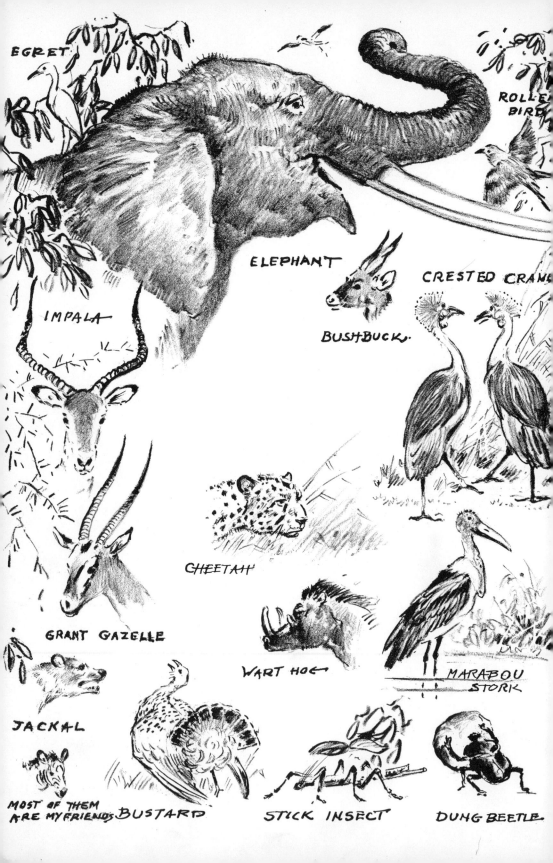

EGRET

ROLLE
BIRD

ELEPHANT

CRESTED CRANE

IMPALA

BUSHBUCK.

CHEETAH

GRANT GAZELLE

WART HOG

MARABOU
STORK

JACKAL

MOST OF THEM
ARE MY FRIENDS

BUSTARD

STICK INSECT

DUNG BEETLE

MOHAMMED, who became the Mighty Mo of this book, was a real elephant. He roamed Northern Kenya for perhaps a century. The country's earliest settlers told of him. Later safaris braved his remote forest haunts to see for themselves, while Africans spun a wealth of folklore about the "Phantom of the North." Little wonder. Mohammed seemed a relic of a past age of titans. He stood twelve feet at the shoulder. One of his enormous tusks measured eleven feet in length.

In 1957, one of East Africa's greatest safari guides, Donald Ker, wrote that "Mohammed must be very, very old." Even as this story was written, the author learned that the aged tusker had died of natural causes in the green depths of his Mount Marsabit forest.

The story, MIGHTY MO, unfolds in a part of Tanganyika the author visited and loved. The places are real, even to the big hollow baobab tree. Jay's father is like many game rangers in today's East Africa, struggling to save wildlife in an era of change that sees wild animals vanishing like America's bison and passenger pigeon. The wildlife area near Lake Manyara is now a national park. Long may it survive with its elephants and million other wonders.

CHAPTER ONE

Elephant Trouble

A small greenish monkey peered from its perch on a tree limb over the stream. Its head was cocked on one side. Its long tail made an arch. The monkey was loudly scolding the boy who splashed in the stream pool below.

Jay Clifford, the game ranger's son, his face dripping, grinned up at the monkey. The light of Africa's quick dawn poked through the leaves, turning the ripples all silver and pink.

"I'll splash all I like." Jay shouted to the monkey. "So you needn't sit there and scowl. Today's special, old monkey. *Special,* do you hear?"

Jay dived headfirst beneath a waterfall, then paddled to the stream's bank, where he sat watching the monkey. "You want to know why today's special?" he went on. "All right then, since you ask me, I'll tell you."

Jay stopped to laugh at the serious look on the monkey's wrinkled face.

"Today is special because we have a guest coming. For a whole month, too! She's my cousin."

The monkey scurried up a branch into the treetops, making brisk little "chit-chit-chit" noises. Jay called after it. "That's not all! When she comes, we're all going on safari to Lake Manyara."

Jay fell silent. He watched the waterfall spraying and thought about the days ahead. What would cousin Suzannah be like? She was eleven, just a year younger than he was. She had lived all her life in London, so he had never met her. What would she think of the part of Africa where the Cliffords lived? It was wild animal country except for the tiny African *shambas* where farming tribes forced corn and cassava to rise from dry poor soil. There were no paved roads, no telephones.

Jay picked up a small stone and tossed it into the water, watching the ripples circle wide. If only his cousin could have been a boy! Then his father might take them on some of his "working" safaris. Those were the adventurous ones—on foot, in rough country.

He tossed a second pebble, harder. "I can track as well as Bogo can," he murmured aloud. "Almost, anyhow."

A third stone struck the water. Jay gave a start. He had not thrown it. He glanced up at the trees, thinking it had been monkey mischief. Then he heard a ripple of laughter behind him.

Jay whirled around to find himself watched by two laughing African boys in long reddish cloaks.

12

"Sangale! Oriono!" cried Jay gladly.

They were a few years older than Jay, old enough to be young *moran,* or warriors. Still, the three boys were good friends. Sangale and Oriono wore their long red hair in tiny tight braids which were drawn together in two tassels —one tassel falling down the neck and the other over the shoulder. Ochre reddened their hair until it was the color of their loose-hanging robes.

Still chuckling over their joke, Sangale and Oriono joined Jay on the stream bank.

"You are not watchful today," murmured Sangale. "If we had been leopards you would have been sorry."

Oriono planted a long gleaming lion spear into the bank beside him. "We came to bring news," he announced.

Jay glanced at his friends in puzzled surprise. "What's happened? Tell me quick."

"Oh, it is nothing that the Masai care about," said Sangale with a lazy yawn. "But the farmers in the village are angry this morning. An elephant wandered among their *shambas.* They say your father must find him and shoot him!"

Jay sprang to a kneeling position, his eyes wide. "Was there damage? Was anybody hurt? Sangale, tell me about it. Oh, Oriono . . . please . . . when was it?"

The two boys only grinned as if amused. Their people were wandering cattle raisers and scorned the farmers. If an elephant raided crops, it meant nothing to the

Masai. But Jay's father had the job of protecting farmers when wild animals caused trouble.

"It happened just this morning," said Oriono.

"They say he was a big one. They say his tusks measured three arms in length."

"*Three* arms!" exclaimed Jay, his eyes growing wide. "Oh it's not so! There's no elephant that big any more . . . not around here."

"I only tell you what the farmers say," shrugged Sangale. "You should go down to the village. They tell about it at the *duka*."

"Is your father still in Arusha?" asked Oriono.

Jay nodded. "He went to meet my cousin and bring her here. He'll be back by noonday."

"What will he do?" asked Oriono, arranging his red cloak over his knees. "Will he lead an elephant hunt?"

Jay frowned and snapped a twig in two. "I don't know. Maybe he'll have to."

"Then you will go too!" said Oriono, showing excitement for the first time. "In our tribe, I have proved my courage by hunting lions. So has Sangale. In the same way you will meet the test of an elephant hunt."

Sangale rose to his knees. "Ehh, yes. And then you'll take hairs from the elephant's tail for good luck. Perhaps you will save some for us."

Oriono's eyes flashed. "I would give you a spear in trade for them."

Jay eyed Oriono's fine lion spear—the long gleaming blade, the smooth shaft. It would be a proud possession. He sighed. "I'd like a spear like that. But I don't know if I'd shoot an elephant."

Eagerness fled from the Masai faces. They stared silently. Jay knew they thought his words were a sign of cowardice. They thought he was afraid to face an elephant. Anger burned deep.

"I *saw* an elephant die once!" Jay spoke darkly. "Some poachers had shot him with poisoned arrows. He just lay there suffering and dying with all the poison in him. When Dad and I got there, people were just laughing and measuring his tusks to see how much money they'd bring. It made me sick."

Jay shredded a leaf, his fingers almost trembling. He knew his words hadn't helped. The two boys did not understand. It was hard—hard to be thought a coward because he wanted animals to live. Of course, nobody thought his father lacked courage. He had shot many elephants. But always, it was because it had to be done. Always, there had been no other choice.

Then Jay remembered the reason Sangale and Oriono had come. He pushed to his feet, snatching his shirt from a bush. "I'm going down to the village to find out about the raid on the *shambas*. Will you come?"

Sangale and Oriono shook their heads. They were happy to stay by the cool of the stream. Jay darted through the bushes alone, slipping his arms into the sleeves of his

16

shirt as he ran. His feet skipped stones, his hands shoved branches aside. Brilliant green lovebirds swirled from acacia bushes, but Jay hardly noticed.

Soon he ducked off the wooded path, and his bare toes dug into the red dust of the Mto-Wa-Mbu village road. Morning sun burned the back of his neck. African women wearing lengths of bright-colored cloth waved to him as he passed. Everyone knew the game ranger's son.

The dirt road led into the village. Tiny Mto-Wa-Mbu had the only store, or *duka,* for many miles around. Safaris stopped here for gasoline and food. Africans came on foot to buy cloth and grain.

Two men from India owned the *duka.* It was a ramshackle old building with a creaky porch and a rusty tin roof. It tilted toward the shade of an aged fig tree. Jay skipped the two steps that led onto the porch and ducked into the shadowy coolness of the store. In a dusty showcase were bubblegum, hairpins, blue beads, and tins of biscuits.

A doorway behind the counter led to a back room. Two men stood in the doorway, watching and listening as something went on beyond. One was Sam, who partly owned the *duka.* The other was a lean African who wore the khaki uniform of the Tanganyika Game Department. It was Bogo, his father's best scout.

Jay slipped behind the counter. Both men turned to nod in greeting as he pressed between them.

"Morning, Sam," whispered Jay breathlessly. He

17

glanced up at Bogo. "Sangale and Oriono just told me there was an elephant raid!"

Bogo waved a hand toward the back room. "You may listen for yourself. The elephant did no harm, but the farmers are angry, angry."

Jay peered into the back room of the store, a favorite meeting place. Nearly a dozen Africans stood in a circle, talking excitedly. Others watched from aside. Some were neatly dressed in khaki trousers and work shirts. Some were shabby and shoeless. A dingy skylight threw a patch of sun on the clay floor where mangos and other fruit had been spread out to ripen. There was a buzzing of flies.

"*N'dio* (yes)," one farmer said, raising his arms over his head. "He came out of the forest making a sound like thunder. His ears were like great wings and his trumpeting ripped grasses from the earth."

Murmurs rose and fell as the others listened. In the corner, a goat had been tied to a water drum. It bleated loudly, and a child began to cry.

"The rogue will bring trouble!" exclaimed another farmer, in a loud voice.

"He must be killed. The game ranger must hunt him!"

Everyone began talking at once. Jay turned to Bogo. "Bogo, let's go have a look at the elephant's tracks! I'll bet we still could find them!"

Bogo spoke quietly. "I have already seen the tracks. Besides, it is for your father to decide when you may track elephants."

18

Jay felt a pang of disappointment. Then Sam's big frame blocked the doorway as he leaned down to speak. Sam was a broad-shouldered *Sikh* with a thick black beard. He wore a blue turban around his head. Pressing a large hand on Jay's shoulder he said in a friendly way, "There is more to be learned about this elephant than the size of his footprints. My brother, Suli, knows more than these farmers. More, even, than Bogo."

Bogo gave a good-natured chuckle. "Eh, that old man, Suli . . . he tells tales like a child."

"What does he say?" asked Jay in surprise. "What could Suli know about the elephant?"

Jay wandered from the store, hands shoved into his pockets. Outside, the brilliant sun made him blink.

Bump. Bumpety-bump.

Nearby, on the rickety *duka* porch, an elderly and wrinkled man hunched over an old-fashioned treadle sewing machine. A dingy violet turban had slipped down over his forehead as he bent over his work. It was Suli, Sam's brother. He was part-owner of the *duka,* but he was also the village tailor.

Jay liked the old *Sikh,* and knew that his nearly deaf ears often caught more news than good ones. He had wisdom, too. It was true Suli loved to make up stories, but Jay could usually tell.

Crossing the porch, Jay stood over Suli until he blocked the sun from the Indian's work. Only then did

20

Suli look up. He grinned. His dark wrinkled face looked like a buttered walnut.

"Ahh, so it is you, mischief?"

Suli loved to tease. Even more, he loved other people to tease him in return. It was custom to insult and tease and fuss with Suli before settling down to talk about anything serious.

"Hey, old Suli!" cried Jay. "You are sewing backward and upside down. A baboon wouldn't wear that rag you are making."

Suli's thin shoulders shook with delighted laughter, but he pretended to be insulted. "Little jackal! Those who wear dust instead of shoes should not insult those who make fine clothes. Remove thy feet from beneath the sewing machine. They soil the cloth!"

Jay pulled an empty wooden crate close to Suli's better ear. His words were serious now. He told of the elephant.

"I have heard," Suli said with a nod, "I have heard what they say. But there is no cause for such alarm. It is not the first time this *tembo* has come down from the forest to walk among men."

Jay's eyes widened in surprise. "Not the first time?" he echoed. "Do you mean this same elephant has come before?"

Suli stopped talking long enough to rearrange his turban, then went on. "Years ago, before your father came here, an elephant with great tusks had a habit of

21

wandering through the village. His footprints were in the dust before this very porch. Most people have forgotten, but I remember it well."

Suli paused to thread a needle with knotted fingers. "He was a young bull elephant. He was curious about human beings and would wander among them once in a while. I think he grew lonely. You see, he belonged to no herd. He came in peace. Never did he do harm. Never to the crops. Never to man, woman, or child. But now . . . now . . . those who remember are gone."

"Oh Suli," cried Jay. "You're telling some kind of made-up tale!"

"Eh?" Suli responded, knitting his leathery brows and leaning closer.

"I *said* . . . I *think* you're *making up a tale!*" shouted Jay.

Suli pretended anger. "Does the fool's tongue of salt blacken the wise man's words of silver? Ah then, I will tell thee no more."

Suli bent over his sewing machine. Thump. Thump. Bumpety-bump. The treadle pumped up and down. The turban slipped out of place, this time over one ear. But the tailor could not bear to be silent for long. Soon he returned to his story.

"He was called Mohammed. Mighty Mohammed. Of course, one cannot be sure this is the same *tembo*. The one that came this morning, I mean. But I, for one, believe it is the same. They talk of his size. Mohammed was this big.   They talk of the length of his tusks and the way they curve.   My mind recalls Mohammed."

As he listened, Jay's wonder grew.   He gazed past the porch and the village.   A red road twisted up, up, up, as it climbed the forested Rift Wall.   Mto-Wa-Mbu nestled in the shadow of highlands like a dusty speck at a green giant's foot.

Up there, though!   Elephants wandered among those trees.   Jay felt excitement stir, and his bare toes curled against the dusty splinters of the plank flooring.   He imagined a giant elephant with sweeping tusks lifted high.

CHAPTER TWO

Suzannah

The sun reached for the noonday center of the sky as Jay hurried home. The Cliffords lived near the village, in a white house half-hidden among trees. He took a short cut and clambered over a low terrace wall.

A big gnarled tree shaded the terrace in front of the ranger's house. A wooden seat encircled its trunk. From the seat came the chatter of Jay's pet monkey, Moppet.

Moppet was a small moustached Guenon monkey that Jay's father had brought home from West Africa. She was olive-green with tufts of bright yellow hair at either side of her face. A broad dash of white just under her nose looked exactly like a moustache.

The little monkey scrambled joyfully across the terrace to Jay. The boy scooped her up and cuffed her playfully. He started for the door, Moppet on one shoulder. Then he stopped short, gasping with surprise. His father's safari car was parked by the house.

"They're here! Dad's home already! And I was supposed to wash and change to clean clothes for Suzannah."

Jay was covered with grime, dust, and dampness. He had been eating a juicy mango from the store. Its stickiness covered his face and arms, along with bits of leaves and smears of dirt. A ripped shirt hung loose over stained trousers that had been chopped off raggedly above the knees.

Letting Moppet scramble away, Jay hurried toward the green safari car. Parcels and purchases waited to be unloaded. A new tire for the Land-Rover. Household supplies from shops in Arusha.

Then Jay's eyes fell on a hat box. It had peppermint stripes and a pink ribbon tied in a fluffy bow. The hat box looked out of place on the dusty green seat, like a frosted teacake on a forest stump. Jay tucked some heavier bundles under one strong arm. Then, with one finger, he hooked the hat box by its ribbon and stared at a neatly printed tag. The box belonged to Suzannah Maguire.

26

"What's anyone going to do with fancy hats in this part of Africa?" he asked himself. "Oh well! Like Mum says, Suzannah's used to cities."

Jay stepped inside the house. He could hear pans clattering in the kitchen as Willy, the Cliffords' house-boy, fixed lunch. He saw no sign of his parents.

Jay could see the guest-room door near the end of the hallway that cut through the house from front to back. As he stood uncertainly in the hall, the door cracked open. A slim girl with large dark eyes and a thin pale face stepped out. Her straight black hair fell to the shoulders of a crisply ironed blue dress. She gave Jay a startled look and stopped short, one hand still on the doorknob.

"Hello there!" Jay called out cheerfully. "You're Suzannah, I guess. Well, I'm Jay Clifford."

For a moment, Jay thought the girl would duck back into the room. Her eyes made him think of shy little dik-diks that darted into the bushes at the least shiver of a leaf. Then she took a hesitant step forward.

"I'm ever so glad to meet you," said Suzannah in a polite voice. She eyed the striped hat box in Jay's grimy fingers. She frowned. "Thank you for bringing my hat. If you'll give it to me, I'll take it to my room before it gets . . . I mean . . . ."

"You mean before it gets all dirty!" Jay finished the sentence, feeling slightly annoyed.

Just then, leaves rustled outside the front door. It was

27

Moppet. The monkey scurried through the door, into the hall. Jay glanced laughingly over his shoulder as Moppet hopped to a table. But his mirth soon ended.

Moppet rested on the table for less than a second. With a sudden stream of cheery chatter, she leaped to her favorite perch on Jay's shoulder. Dismay clouded Suzannah's face, but it was too late. Moppet's quick and playful hand grabbed for a lock of the girl's long hair.

Suzannah gave a loud cry. She shrank back, covering her face with both arms. "Get that thing away from me! Get it away!"

Footsteps hurried toward the hall. Jay's mother and father appeared, just as Moppet dashed for the front door. Mrs. Clifford drew Suzannah into her arms. Looking at Jay in alarm, his mother asked, "What on earth happened?"

"It was just Moppet," Jay explained. "She . . . all she did was to pull Suzannah's hair a little bit."

Jay's father stood in the doorway. He was a tall man with a lean bronzed face and a black moustache. He wore khaki trousers and a loose-fitting bush jacket. Jay hadn't seen his father in several days, but there was no time to greet him now.

"Hush now, Suzannah," said the game ranger firmly. "It was just Jay's pet monkey. She was saying hello in her own way."

Jay's mother soothed Suzannah, pressing her cheek

gently against the dark top of the girl's head. "You shouldn't be frightened of Moppet, dear. Jay has a monkey for a pet . . . just as you might have a dog or a kitten."

"I've never had a pet!" Suzannah retorted, her lips trembling. "I wouldn't want one either. Animals are dirty."

Jay looked from his blond-haired, pretty mother to his tall, deeply tanned father. He was bewildered and speechless.

Later, at lunch, Suzannah apologized for her outburst. Just the same, nobody felt like talking about animals during the meal. Jay shifted restlessly in his chair, longing to talk to his father about the morning's elephant trouble.

Suzannah sat straight and prim, telling about the plane trip from London. Her grown-up way of talking made Jay uncomfortable. She told about her parents, who were archaeologists. Sometimes their work took them to faraway places in search of museum pieces. Suzannah had to stay at home with a governess. Now they were in a little-known part of Africa, so they had decided to let Suzannah visit the Cliffords. Her mother and father would join her when their work was done.

Jay's mother listened and chatted and smiled her soft pretty smile. Jay's mother had a gentle way. It fooled people who didn't know she was as brave as most men. She would creep up on leopards to take pictures. She had driven trucks all alone through roadless bush country to reach safaris in trouble.

30

"Madeleine is ever so nice. She's my governess," Suzannah explained. "I call her 'Madi.' She taught me to play checkers this year. I always beat her, though. Do you play checkers, Jay?"

Jay shook his head.

"I shall teach you," announced Suzannah firmly. "I brought my own set. And we can read aloud to each other. I promised Madi I'd read lots of books because I shall miss two months of school. Where's your school, Jay?"

"With a missionary near here. But he's sick with malaria."

Suzannah shuddered. "Madi says everyone gets awful diseases in Africa if they don't stay out of the sun and take lots of medicine. I have five kinds of pills."

Jay started to say that he'd be more afraid of catching germs in London. Then he caught a warning look from his father and he dug into a bowl of chicken curry instead. The weeks ahead looked dark, indeed. He'd never seen anyone as stiff and serious as Suzannah, not even a grownup. He wondered if she ever had fun.

After lunch, the heat of afternoon found its way into the house. Shades were drawn. In the kitchen and in Suzannah's room, ceiling fans whirred softly. Suzannah took a nap. But out on the terrace, four scouts collected for a meeting with Rob Clifford. The time had come, at last, to talk about the big elephant. Jay slipped from the house to join the group.

Rob Clifford stood beneath the fig tree, one leg propped

on the wooden bench. His eyes had a worried look. Well they might. As game ranger, he had many thousands of miles of countryside to patrol. It was his job to see that laws protecting animals were not broken. Each year the job seemed harder. Big gangs of armed men killed hundreds of wild animals at a time, in traps or with poisoned arrows. Ivory and rhino horn were smuggled out by traders. Black-market meat brought high prices. Giraffe sinews were used for bow strings, and wildebeest tails for fly whisks. Jay's father worked without rest to stop the cruel trade.

The ranger had a second big job. He protected the farmers and their crops from animals that caused trouble.

Now Bogo and three other scouts told of the elephant tracks and the farmers' complaints.

"I didn't know we had a *tembo* that big around here," said the ranger. "For years, people have been killing the big ones or driving them out."

"I did not know it either," answered Bogo. "But I measured the footprints myself."

"Well, I'm itching for a look at this big fellow," said the ranger. "I want to check that country up there for poachers anyway. But we're only going to take a *look* at this elephant. He did no harm to the *shambas*. He is not to be shot . . . not this time."

"The farmers will not be happy, *Bwana*," warned a scout named Big Charlie. "They think he will return for evil."

32

"If he returns for evil, then he must pay for evil. But let's give him another chance. All right?"

"It is true that he raided no crops this time," said Bogo. "But why did he come?"

Jay could be still no longer. "Suli said that an elephant like this one used to visit the *shambas* years ago. He was a big lone tusker. He was just . . . well . . . maybe curious or lonely. He never did any harm."

"Suli said that?" queried the ranger, raising his eyebrows. "Oh well, he makes up stories sometimes, Jay."

"I'm sure he wasn't making this one up," protested Jay. "He described him. It sounded just like the elephant the farmers are talking about. It's possible, after all!"

"Of course, it's possible," agreed the ranger. "Anyhow, I'd like to have a look at this big tusker . . . and some poachers." He turned to his scouts. "We'll leave in an hour. I expect we'll be on safari three nights."

Last orders were given and the three scouts slipped away, one by one, to prepare for the trip.

"I'm sorry you can't come," said Jay's father, when the last man had vanished down the path. "I know how much you want to. But this is going to be a troublesome 'go.' "

Jay kicked at the terrace wall and watched a chameleon as it made a slow, slow path between two flower pots.

"What you mean is, I've got to stay home and be nice to Suzannah."

"It's up to you to help her like Africa," said his father quietly. "As soon as I get back from this trip, I want to take you all on that safari to Lake Manyara. Suzannah will have a chance to see zebras and gazelles . . . and some animal country so pretty she can't hate it."

The next two days passed quietly. Suzannah went no farther from the house than to the edge of the red canna flower bed. She asked permission to weed and water it. She helped with housework, too. Jay's mother said she had never seen a tidier child.

Once, Jay tried to persuade Suzannah to walk as far as the village. She frowned and shook her head stubbornly.

"I saw the village when we came through it," she said. "However do you pronounce that odd name? I shan't bother to try. Anyway, the place looked hot and dirty."

"You'd like old Suli," argued Jay. "He's got stories to tell. Not just about Africa, either. About *India,* where he was born."

For a moment, Suzannah looked interested. She was arranging flowers in a vase. She stopped and peered over them at Jay. "I don't know why he ever left India for this place. You keep talking about elephants. I've read that elephants in India are tame. People can *ride* them, and it's much more civ . . . civilized."

"Indian elephants!" Jay hissed his scorn. "Those dumb old things let themselves be handled like a lot of cows. You've never seen an elephant 'til you've seen an African tusker. Naturally nobody tames them. They're wild and they belong that way."

Suzannah shrugged and jabbed a flower stem into the vase. "Well, I hope there won't be any around at Lake . . . Lake whatever-it's-called where Uncle Rob is taking us on a safari."

"Well, I hope there *are!*" retorted Jay. "Matter of fact, it's a good place to find them. Rhinos, too. And lions."

Jay saw Suzannah's lips quiver. He knew he had frightened her, but he didn't care.

"In that case," Suzannah said slowly, "I expect Uncle Rob will take lots of guns to protect us. Do you know how to shoot a gun, Jay? I . . . I don't at all."

"Naturally, I know how," boasted Jay. "I can almost handle Dad's .470. That's his biggest elephant gun."

Suzannah forgot the flowers. She stared wide-eyed. "Have you ever shot an elephant?"

"Well . . . no," admitted Jay. He didn't add that he had never killed any kind of animal. "But I could if I had to. I've practiced enough. But I don't know why you're always talking about shooting animals. Dad's job is to protect them."

Suzannah shook her head, puzzled. "Even lions?"

"Especially lions. They're getting rare because so many have been killed. Dad says there aren't even half as many lions in Africa as there were when he first came."

Suzannah seemed thoughtful. Then she faced Jay with a challenging gleam in her eyes. "What would you do if you came face to face with that big elephant . . . the one that scared everyone the day I came? Everyone's afraid of him. I heard Willy say so! What would you do?"

Jay fumbled for the right answer. Suzannah had him on the spot. Hadn't he himself been wondering what he would do?

"If I *had* to shoot him, I would!" Jay burst out.

Suddenly, in his anger, he found he meant it.

CHAPTER THREE

Smudge

Ranger Clifford returned three days later. Wearily he pulled off his walking boots, rubbed stinging eyes, and shook his head. "No elephants with three-arm-long tusks. No poachers caught. A notably unsuccessful trip."

He was eager to start for Lake Manyara with his family and Suzannah. "That'll be like vacation to me," he grinned. "Soft travel in lorries, sleeping in tents."

By dawn of the next day, the small safari raised clouds of red dust from the road. The ranger's sturdy Land-Rover led, with Jay in the front seat and two scouts in the rear. They took off its canvas top and latched the front glass against the hood. Jay clutched his felt hat as the warm wind and dust hit his face.

The safari car followed, with Suzannah, Mrs. Clifford, two more scouts, and Willy inside. The rear was tightly packed with tents, food, and other supplies.

Farms and thatched huts fell behind. The road nar-

rowed through a countryside of tall yellowed grasses and scrubby acacia trees. Jay watched a family of wart hogs scurry stiffly out of the way, their bristly snouts upturned as if they thought themselves royalty.

A gerenuk doe, its slender legs planted in the side of a four-foot anthill, turned its strange long neck to watch. The doe's eyes blended into upswept dark stripes on its face, so that the slanted eyes seemed huge.

Dry open country deepened into cool forest near the river. A herd of impala were feeding among the trees. Sun through branches dappled coppery coats. Soft dark eyes grew wary as the Land-Rover and safari car drew near.

Then the impala were gone. Land-Rover and safari car rattled over a rickety bridge. Rhino tracks marked the forest road. At last, grasslands stretched ahead, yellow beneath the blue sky. To the right, the forested Rift Wall sloped steeply to the highlands above. To the left, grasslands deepened gradually into the swamplands of Lake Manyara!

Jay pointed excitedly to the first herd of zebras. Each striped head lifted, wary of the rumbling and smell of the oncoming lorries. An old bull wildebeest shook his massive, bearded forequarters and, startled, ran in circles.

Rob Clifford had chosen a camping place near an ancient baobab tree. It overlooked the grasslands like a sentinel. Its huge, twisted trunk was bigger around than the Land-Rover and safari car together.

Jay hurried to help unload tent rolls from the safari car. "How do you like it here?" he asked, grinning at Suzannah.

Suzannah was gripping the rear seat with both hands as if afraid of leaving it. Her face barely showed under the floppy brim of a straw sun hat. She was wearing a shortened pair of Jay's trousers because she had brought no clothes sturdy enough for African camping. "Aren't there any houses or other people?" stammered Suzannah.

Jay chuckled. "We brought our own houses. Wait 'til you see your tent. We got it new last year and it even has a front porch. Here. Grab an end of this roll and help unload."

Suzannah didn't budge. She was staring beyond the baobab tree. "Who's that man talking with Uncle Rob?"

As Jay glanced around, the tent roll went forgotten. "It's Daniel! One of Dad's scouts. I almost forgot he was meeting us here. He's been looking for elephants!"

Jay darted away. A moment later he was beside his father, listening to news brought by the scout.

Daniel came from a proud hunting tribe. He had spent more of his life among wild animals than among people. He could move so quietly even a bushbuck couldn't hear him. His ears were keen enough to hear a beetle crawling over a leaf. He spoke softly in his own tongue, using few words.

"I find signs of the big elephant, *Bwana*," he was saying. He motioned over his shoulder. "South part of forest. He travels with a second elephant. Much smaller bull."

Jay's eyes widened. "Did you see them?"

Daniel shook his head. "Only prints. Trees broken by elephants."

Rob Clifford rubbed the back of his neck thoughtfully. "So there are two of them. Well, it's not surprising. Big tuskers often have an *askari* tagging along."

"*Askari?*" queried Jay. "That means a guard elephant, doesn't it? He's one who's forever following a big tusker?"

41

"That's right," answered Bogo. "It's often so with big bulls that travel apart from a herd. And the *askari* feels important to be with such a grand friend."

"I find one other thing, *Bwana*," Daniel said in a voice hardly above a whisper.

Without another word, the scout turned toward the baobab tree. Jay and his father glanced after him in surprise, then followed. The tree's big trunk was partly hollow, with an opening large enough for a man. Daniel ducked inside. As Jay bent by the opening, he could see only shadowy darkness inside. Then he heard scuffling sounds.

Daniel's head popped from the tree. Then his lanky frame slipped out. In his arms, kicking and frightened, was a baby zebra.

Jay stared in wordless amazement. Rob Clifford whistled long and low. From the camp site, Jay heard his mother's cry of surprise. She stopped opening crates and hurried to join them.

Daniel laid his small burden on the grass. The zebra was only a few weeks old. Perfectly formed stripes showed beneath a baby coat of brownish fuzz. Round furry ears were black-rimmed. A delicate nose, black and soft, quivered with frightened little breaths. The little animal was thin from hunger.

"Poachers killed its mother," murmured Daniel. "I found her in a wire snare, and the little one nearby. Perhaps you can save him."

Jay and his mother had already knelt close to the little animal. "He's almost starved," said Jay, feeling ribs beneath the striped sides.

Suzannah had left the safari car. Jay noticed her

standing behind him. Clutching the brim of her sun hat with both hands she stared down. "What is that?" she demanded. "Won't it bite?"

"Of course it won't!" retorted Jay. "The poor little animal is too weak to do anything at all. It's a baby zebra."

Suzannah pressed closer, bending cautiously for a better view. The little zebra seemed to stare up at her. First Suzannah was wide-mouthed and speechless. Then she spoke with a quaver in her voice. "Why . . . it's like a little toy animal. It's all fuzzy."

Willy had already built a campfire as he fixed lunch. Soon he appeared beneath the baobab tree, a saucer of warmed milk in his hand. He looked down at the little newcomer and shook his head sadly. "He must eat."

"I don't know how we're going to feed him," said Jay with a worried frown. "We need a bottle with a nipple."

"Won't he drink from the bowl?" asked Suzannah.

"Course not. He wouldn't know how," answered Jay.

The baby zebra lay crumpled and limp on the grass, its eyes shut. Bogo and Big Charlie left their work to look. "He is too weak. He cannot live," said Bogo.

Jay and his mother tried to dribble the warm milk into the little animal's mouth with their hands. They tried to make him suck it from their fingers. They coaxed; they held his head, and tried forcing it down. Jay held the soft neck against his arm. He could feel the zebra's fright.

At last Jay sat back on his heels, brushing away some

flies that hovered over the cooling milk. "Maybe he'd be better off if we left him alone for a while."

"I think you're right," answered his mother, brushing some spilled milk from her tan trousers. She glanced up at Suzannah. "How would you like to keep an eye on him, dear? Jay and I should be helping to set up camp."

"Me?" Suzannah looked startled. "I . . . I wouldn't know what to do."

Mrs. Clifford found an empty green food crate and drew it close. "Just sit here. It's nice and cool under the tree. You only have to watch our little patient and call us if he seems worse."

Suzannah shrugged. "Well, if you say I must, Aunt June. . . ."

Jay looked at his cousin carefully. He had a hunch she wasn't as displeased as she pretended to be.

Jay helped his father and Bogo drive tent pegs. Soon a row of green tents stood crisp and taut-roofed on the grass. The middle tent was largest. It held a long table and crates of supplies. Chairs and smaller tables lined the canvas walls. Makeshift shelves held water jugs, cameras, books, and lanterns. Through the wide-open front tent flap, Jay could see the plains all the way to the edge of the swamp.

Smaller sleeping tents flanked the big one. Jay would share one with his father. Suzannah and Mrs. Clifford had the newest one. Both tents had canvas-roofed front "porches" with folding tables and chairs.

More than an hour later, camp was nearly complete. Willy had set the table for lunch. Jay worked with a rag, dusting the big wireless that brought them news broadcasts from Nairobi. Suddenly, Suzannah burst into the tent. She stopped just inside, and Jay turned to notice an excited sparkle in her eyes.

"If you please. I need some more warm milk," said Suzannah. Her face was flushed deep red from the sun's heat and her own hurry.

Jay blinked in surprise. "More milk?" he echoed.

"Yes. More milk. Are you stupid? I thought I spoke clearly. I need some *more warm milk*. I've figured out how to make the baby zebra eat." Suzannah was trying to hide her eager excitement by acting annoyed at Jay. Then she held up one hand, waving a small glass object.

Jay's mouth dropped open. He stared. "What is it?"

"A medicine dropper, of course. Don't be so dumb."

Jay clapped his hands as he understood. "Why, that's it! That's just the thing we need! Suzie, you're brilliant!"

Willy reheated some milk. Together Suzannah and Jay hurried back to the baobab tree. Soon Suzannah was busy dipping the glass tip of the dropper into the milk and squeezing the rubber handle to fill it. The baby zebra lay between them, his head on Jay's knee.

Jay helped support the small striped neck while Suzannah slipped the dropper into the animal's mouth. "You won't be able to use it for any nose drops after it's all

46

gooeyed up with milk and dribbling," he said mischievously.

Suzannah didn't answer. She was too busy. Again and again, she emptied the dropper into the small mouth. Jay held the graceful head until he felt swallowing.

"It works," Jay cried softly. "It really works."

Suzannah's eyes flashed triumphantly. She stopped to rest, brushing at some milk that had spilled on her knee. Timidly she stroked the bumpy place between the little zebra's eyes. "What a funny smudgy nose he has," she murmured. "Just as if he'd dipped it into some charcoal." She paused, and her voice had a wistful note. "If he were mine, that's what I'd call him. Smudge."

Jay grinned to himself. He didn't remind Suzannah that only a few days before she'd vowed she wouldn't want a pet. Instead, he exclaimed, "Smudge! That's a cracking good name, Suzie. It's just right."

Suzannah smiled in a pleased way. Then she became thoughtful. "Why did the men make traps to kill Smudge's mother?" she asked.

"Just so they could sell the meat illegally. Poachers would kill all the animals in the Province if it weren't for people like Dad. But say! I thought you didn't care about animals."

"Smudge is different!" Suzannah retorted stubbornly.

CHAPTER FOUR

Animals Everywhere Around

At lunch, Suzannah said she had fed Smudge only to please Aunt June and Uncle Rob. Jay knew his cousin was pretending. She couldn't stop glancing at the baby zebra. He had been nested down under a corner table.

Suzannah almost forgot to take her yellow pills as she fussed over Smudge. Usually she talked about how important they were.

A lazy afternoon passed, humming with flies. The scouts and Willy slept. Hot sun burned the flat tops of acacia trees on the grasslands. Jay explored the bushy edge of the campsite and found a six-inch "stick" insect for a collection he kept at home.

Camp and the plains came to life as the sun dipped low. The grasslands turned gold. The "quaag quaag" of zebras seemed a welcome for the approaching coolness.

Jay and his father loaded binoculars and cameras into the safari car. Suzannah tied her hair in a big kerchief to protect it from dust. Late afternoon was the time to see animals. Soon the car was bumping across roadless grasslands. Graceful Grant gazelles watched it with brilliant dark eyes. Zebras scattered before the lorry, wheeling to show their chubby hindquarters.

Mr. Clifford slowed to a stop not far from a grove of acacia trees. He pointed at something and whispered, *"Twiga."*

"What does *twiga* mean?" asked Suzannah, staring into the trees ahead.

"That's a Swahili word for a certain kind of animal," answered Jay. "But I won't tell you. Look sharp. You'll see."

The ranger cut the noisy engine. The trees seemed a quiet tangle of branches, shadowy and without life. Suzannah frowned impatiently. "I don't see a single thing."

"One . . . two. Three *twiga!*" Jay counted them off in a teasing voice. "Four. Five of them. One's just a youngster."

Mrs. Clifford leaned close to Suzannah, pointing for her. "Watch. Right there. Through the crotch of that tree. *Twiga* have wonderful color protection. To see them is sometimes like solving a puzzle."

Suddenly Suzannah gave a long astonished gasp. Her eyes grew huge. "Gi . . . gi . . . *giraffes!*"

Two long necks poked above the treetops. Until they moved, the necks seemed part of the trees. Then one giraffe bent gracefully for a nibble of acacia leaves. Another stared solemnly toward the safari car. It stood so close Jay could see its thick black lashes flicker above gentle eyes. An Ox-bird lit between the bumpy horns.

Long legs moved quietly among the trees. Then the giraffes took fright. They seemed to drift from the trees as

if carried by a secret wind. Once in the clear, they moved off with a rocking gallop, single file. Their long legs reached easily, almost lazily, as if in time to slow music. But they covered the grasslands with amazing speed and soon were slender silhouettes against an amber sky.

Once more the safari car moved on. A pair of jackals slipped into the bushes. A lilac-breasted roller bird eyed the car from a branch, then flitted away. Jay glimpsed a cheetah, but it vanished too quickly for Suzannah's untrained eyes.

"What are those *things?*" demanded Suzannah, pointing at a herd of grayish animals not far away. "They look like strange old horses with beards and horns."

Everyone laughed. "They're wildebeests," explained Mr. Clifford. "And look over there. A bustard."

An immense black and white bird plodded along, feathers puffed. It looked like a pompous old man.

By the time they returned to camp, the sun had dropped behind the Rift Wall. It looked black and more massive than ever. Shadows beyond the tents wrapped the zebras out of view, leaving only their barking calls to prove they

were still there. Willy lit kerosene lamps and blocked tent openings with mosquito netting.

Suzannah watched the gathering darkness with anxious eyes. "I feel animals everywhere around. But now we can't see them. It's scary."

Mrs. Clifford smoothed her niece's hair. "First night

on safari even scares grown men sometimes. Don't worry. Just remember that the animals are more afraid of us than we are of them. They're not going to come near a pack of noisy people, with all their smelly equipment and blazing campfires."

During dinner, hyenas cackled and simpered from the shadows beyond the campfire glow.

"They won't come any closer," said Jay encouragingly.

Suzannah chewed her lower lip doubtfully. "Bogo said a hyena would attack a baby zebra. Oh Aunt June! Could we keep Smudge in our tent tonight?"

CHAPTER FIVE

Mohammed and the Askari

At dawn, Willy blew out the kerosene lamps and fed the campfire with fresh logs to make tea. Jay carried warm water to the sleeping tents and filled canvas wash basins.

Work done, Jay gazed out on the grasslands. The air was still cool. Tiny birds filled the grasses with chatter. Not far away, a herd of Thomson gazelles grazed. As he watched, Suzannah joined him. There was not a crease in her khaki trousers. Her face looked freshly scrubbed. Her hair fell smooth, shiny, and combed, to her shoulders.

"How's Smudge?" asked Jay anxiously.

"Why, he's so strong this morning I can hardly believe it!" answered Suzannah, smiling. "Come look. But be quiet. Aunt June is still sleeping."

Jay followed his cousin to the tent and lifted the flap. Just inside, Smudge was standing with his legs braced apart, as if still shaky. But his eyes were bright and bold.

"He's hungry again!" whispered Suzannah. "He's been

greedy as a pig. The medicine dropper's not big enough any more. I fed him most of the night."

"How could you sleep and feed him most of the night?" Jay ducked out of the tent, Suzannah behind him.

"I couldn't sleep hardly at all . . . 'cause of all the noises. I heard lions! And things howling."

Jay grinned. "The things howling were bush-babies. They live in trees and they're cute little things with huge eyes

and soft fur. Harmless. As for lions . . . well, I heard them, too. But you'll come to like the sound."

"I will not. Not *ever!*" retorted Suzannah.

"Let's go heat some milk for Smudge," suggested Jay, mostly to change the subject.

Jay headed for the campfire behind the tents. Suzannah started to follow, then stopped short. She had glanced back at the plains. "Jay . . . what's that . . . that *thing* moving way over there? It . . . it looks like an animal."

Jay whirled around. His eyes scanned the yellowish grasslands not far from the swamp. Then he drew a sharp breath. "Go get Dad!" he said breathlessly. "He's in the main tent with Daniel and Bogo."

Suzannah seemed pinned to the spot. "What is it?" she asked in a frightened voice.

"Elephant," answered Jay, trying to make his voice matter-of-fact. But his excitement doubled, then redoubled as he watched the moving spot on the grasslands.

Suzannah clapped both hands against her face and stifled a small cry.

"Oh come on!" Jay exclaimed impatiently. "He's almost a mile off and he's not going to hurt you! But never mind, I'll get Dad myself."

Jay wheeled about and dashed toward the main tent. Inside, Rob Clifford bent over a map. Bogo, Daniel, and Big Charlie were with him.

"*Tembo!*" cried Jay. "Near the lake. Right in the open!"

The ranger whirled from his chair and reached the tent opening in one quick stride. Binoculars in hand, he gazed toward the plains. The three scouts joined him, murmuring and looking.

"Big one, *Bwana,*" murmured Bogo.

"*N'dio* (yes)," agreed Big Charlie. "Going from swamp toward the forest."

The ranger studied the elephant carefully through his binoculars. His face wore a puzzled look as he lowered them, then handed them to Daniel.

"Look carefully," he said. "Tell me if you've ever seen that elephant before. I thought that after sixteen years I knew most of the *tembos* in this area, and it would be hard to miss a giant like that. Yet I could swear I have never seen him before."

Jay felt his heart thumping. He scarcely breathed as Daniel quietly watched the elephant through the glasses and then handed them to Bogo. "I think it is the big one we have been tracking, *Bwana*," said Daniel quietly.

"Let's go have a closer look," said Ranger Clifford. He strode toward the Land-Rover. Jay fell into step, flushed with excitement. He caught sight of Suzannah near the entrance of her tent. She looked as she had the first time Jay had seen her. Timid as a dik-dik, ready to run.

Jay paused and called out, "Want to come with us? We're going to get a close look at the elephant."

"Are you going to shoot it?"

"Of course not," answered Rob Clifford. "Unless we shoot a *picture* of it. That's the best kind of shooting for a pretty morning like this."

Suzannah shook her head. "I'd better stay and feed Smudge."

The Land-Rover engine choked, then purred smoothly. Bogo, Daniel, and Big Charlie crowded into the rear. In a few minutes, they were bouncing over the bumpy plains.

"If we skirt the edge of the bush country we'll have a chance of coming close before he hears the truck. The wind should be with us. Then we can stop and watch," said Rob Clifford.

Jay's eyes were still on the gray shape that moved slowly over the yellow grasslands. He saw the elephant halt its shambling gait. Then he saw the trunk curl up, twist and question the air. Surely the keen ears had already picked up the sound of the Land-Rover engine.

Jay's father noticed the change. He veered into a light grove of acacia trees and cut the engine. In silence they watched through a screen of branches.

The elephant moved closer and closer. What a beauty he was! Jay's heart beat faster as the great ears spread slightly to trap sounds. Now the great animal was only about one hundred yards away. As he turned slightly, Jay could see the full sweeping length of his tusks. The first glimpse of them made Jay gasp, and he heard Bogo's grunt of surprise. The tusks curved only slightly, like great saber swords. But it was the length of them that made Jay feel shivery all over.

Closer and closer. Now nobody spoke. Now any noise might give them away.

The great ears fanned wide, straight out from the elephant's shoulders. He shifted about, raking the air gently with the long tusks. His trunk kept curling and twisting, for his sharp senses told him of an unfamiliar presence.

60

Suddenly, to everyone's surprise, the elephant changed direction. He was coming straight toward the Land-Rover instead of moving at an angle toward the forest. Jay felt Bogo stiffen behind him. Jay knew the wise scout was suddenly on guard and uneasy.

Jay stole a glance at his father. Rob Clifford's eyes had an anxious squint.

It was Big Charlie who murmured the first warning. "I think we better start the engine, *Bwana*," he whispered softly. "That *tembo* might charge us."

The ranger's hand already rested on the starter key. But he hesitated as if he didn't want to break the silence with the engine's noise. Jay's fingers dug into the seat beneath him. His scalp tingled.

The elephant was so close Jay could see the veining on the animal's ears and the rings of heavy creases around his trunk. There was a noble look about his great head. It had hard angles, like carved rock, instead of smooth rounded curves. As he moved, still lazily, he seemed to belong to the land beneath him, to the bushes beyond.

"Don't start the engine yet," Jay whispered, pleading. "I'm sure he'll turn off. Let's have a better look."

But the fanning of the elephant's ears could have been a threat. Rob Clifford shook his head. "I like my trouble after breakfast, not before," he joked, flashing a quick smile. He turned the key.

The engine's roar shattered the stillness.

The huge elephant halted immediately. His ears fanned out to their full span like gray banners unfurled. He was so close Jay could see the greenish black color of his eyes, and the tiny cracks in the long tusks.

Jay was still grabbing a last quick look when Big Charlie cried a warning. Then, like explosions, the sound of crashing trees filled the air. In a flash, Jay thought the big elephant had broken into a charge. But no. He still watched quietly, unmoving.

Then he heard Bogo's cry. "There! A second *tembo!* There, *Bwana!* Look out!"

Directly behind them, a tree crashed down. Jay whirled in his seat. Later, he remembered that he himself had yelled. A one-tusked elephant, ears spread in anger, trunk curled under, bore down upon the Land-Rover. Then the trunk lifted. An ear-splitting blast of enraged trumpeting froze Jay's blood.

Rob Clifford's foot jammed the accelerator to the floor. Jay clutched the seat and held tight as the tires bumped in and out of a ditch, over logs and stones. With seconds to spare, they reached the clearer grasslands and put a safe distance between themselves and the charging elephant.

The one-tusker screamed again, then stopped in its tracks.

Rob Clifford brought the Land-Rover around in a sweeping circle. Once more they faced the gray bush, but now from a distance. For a moment they glimpsed the second elephant. It was a small bull. His one tusk poked bluntly upward from beneath his trunk. Then he turned and slipped out of sight among the broken trees. Now the giant elephant appeared on the same spot. He headed into the shadows just behind the little one-tusker. Following like a huge friendly puppy, he vanished.

Jay was too shaky to speak. All five of them watched quietly until the forest closed completely behind the two elephants.

Suddenly Jay's father relaxed and grinned. "I don't think little 'one-tusk' likes people!"

"We're lucky we didn't get stalled, lumping over that tree stump," Jay breathed.

"I think they are the elephants we have been tracking," said Daniel. "The big one travels with a small *askari* . . . just as the other trails showed."

"They're usually mean, those *askaris,*" added Rob Clifford. "They're the ones who protect the big boss!"

Jay's father shoved the Land-Rover into gear and headed across the peaceful plains. He was looping toward the spot where the big elephant had been seen earlier. Jay knew his father wanted to have a look at the elephant's track. Soon the ranger stopped, pointing to the rough grass ahead. Hopping to the ground, they all bent over the clearest prints.

"Those tracks must be almost twenty inches across!" exclaimed Jay.

Jay's father knelt, studying the ground. "Mighty Mohammed," he murmured.

Jay stared in wide-mouthed surprise. "Dad! You used the name Suli called him. You *do* believe it's the same elephant."

Rob Clifford chuckled, rubbed the back of his neck,

and winked at Jay. "Now you're not to start thinking I swallow all of Suli's tale. But an elephant like that needs a name, after all, and . . . well, who knows? Elephants have turned up stranger surprises."

"Mighty Mohammed," murmured Daniel. "He has seen a long life. I hope we will not have to end his days."

CHAPTER SIX

Smudge Is Lost

Days passed. Nobody saw the big bull elephant or his *askari* companion. No word of new elephant raids had come from the farmers near Mto-Wa-Mbu.

Rob Clifford worked hard, scouting the area for poachers. When he was away, he always left at least one of his scouts in charge of camp. The small group spent early mornings and late afternoons on the plains, studying animals and taking pictures.

Each day Smudge grew stronger. Willy and Big Charlie drove back to Mto-Wa-Mbu twice to buy extra milk for him. The little zebra learned to gulp his meals straight from a lemon soda bottle. He frisked and explored and left a trail of laughter and mischief wherever he went.

And Suzannah laughed, too. More and more. And her sunburn was deepening into a red-brown tan. Her pinched face filled out until Willy began teasing. "I do not know who is hungrier all the time . . . Smudge or the little *memsahib*," he would say.

66

Suzannah's curiosity about wildlife grew each day. Now she could tell the Grant gazelles from the Thomson gazelles. Her favorites were the "tommies," with their licorice-twist horns and their black tassel tails that always switched. She said that a herd of them bounding away looked like people waving good-by with lace handkerchiefs at a train station.

And she loved the saucy zebras. "Isn't there any such thing as a thin, dirty zebra?" she asked. "They always look as if someone had just stuffed them to bursting and painted them fresh. I think someone must do it during the night."

"Why do giraffes always look so uppity?" she queried one morning. "As if they didn't approve of people at all. They make me remember a great aunt of mine who is a countess and who got mad at me once for not wearing white gloves at tea."

Gradually Suzannah lost her fear of the dark African nights. When the weird cackles of hyenas filled the air beyond the campfire's glow, she no longer held her ears.

They had been on safari one week and a day. The sun burned especially hot. After a long morning away from camp, everyone was ready for an afternoon of rest. Rob Clifford was away, and would not return until later.

The afternoon was hot and sleepy, the kind of day that even made the warblers seem to fly with wilted wings. The plains before the tent seemed almost empty of animals. One lone wildebeest trudged sullenly near the swamp. The air smelled of dust.

"It will rain soon," Willy promised, as he packed away the lunch dishes. He glanced toward the sky above the Rift Wall, then vanished to his tent to sleep through the afternoon heat.

"Aunt is sleeping, too," Suzannah told Jay as she wandered into the main tent. "She has a headache from heat."

Jay had some tough elephant-hair strands spread out on the table. He was weaving them into a bracelet. He looked up as he heard the rustle of hoofs on canvas floor cover. Smudge had trotted in behind Suzannah.

"Everyone's asleep," Suzannah went on, "except for you and me. What are you doing?"

"Making a bracelet out of elephant hairs," replied Jay.

"Elephant hairs! How ugly. Besides, I didn't know elephants had hair. Those look like black wire."

"Umm. They're tough as wire, all right. They come out of an elephant's tail. If you were ever that close to an elephant, you'd see them."

"I still think they're ugly," commented Suzannah. "Who's going to wear that, when you're finished?"

"A friend of mine named Oriono. He's a Masai. He might give me a lion spear as a trade."

"Ugg . . . ee. Who wants *that?*"

Jay began wishing Suzannah would leave him in peace with his work. The hairs were slippery and hard to handle. But the girl kept talking.

"Smudge is getting so strong I can hardly hold him," said Suzannah, sitting at the camp table, her chin in her hands. "I'm starting to wonder if we shouldn't tie him up when we leave camp. Or else take him along."

"Tie him up!" exclaimed Jay, dropping a handful of hairs. "You wouldn't do that to the poor thing, would you? He'd be miserable."

"But Jay. I'm afraid a lion will get him. Or a hyena or leopard. Bogo says that hundreds of animals will pounce on a baby zebra quicker'n you can say 'scoot,' as soon as he gets into some bush . . . or practically anywhere away from camp."

Jay frowned at his work. He knew Suzannah had reason to worry. Baby zebras were easy prey for many animals. Even while they talked, Smudge had trotted from the tent and headed for the open plains. Suzannah jumped up and darted after him.

Glad to be alone, Jay picked up the stiff strands of elephant hair once more. He bent close to his work, his fingers struggling with loops and knots. He could hear Suzannah scolding as she pulled the mischievous wanderer back to camp. Then Jay forgot about Suzannah and Smudge until half an hour later. He heard his cousin calling him from behind the tents.

"Jay! Jay! Smudge is wandering again. Come help me get him back."

"Oh . . . crikety crikety crow!" muttered Jay impatiently. His forehead puckered in a frown, for he was tying the last of the complicated knots that would finish the bracelet. If he dropped the work now, it would come apart. He tried to hurry, but his haste made his fingers clumsy.

Suzannah didn't call again. Jay decided she must have caught Smudge. He would finish the knot and then make sure. But he forgot.

Long minutes passed before Jay thought of Suzannah and Smudge again. Now the very silence among the tents seemed a warning that something was amiss.

It was too quiet!

Jay hopped to his feet and went out into the sunlight. When had he last heard Suzannah? Bogo and Willy were asleep. Only the buzzing of some flies around the tent entrance broke the heavy silence.

At that moment, he heard a thin voice calling from far away. "Smudge. Please, Smudge. Come here."

The calls came from deep in the bush behind the tent clearing. Suzannah had wandered from camp, alone.

70

Jay broke into a run. Taller grasses that fringed the tent clearing brushed his knees. The thick undergrowth and thorn bushes closed around him. He ducked, shielding his face as he ran. It was risky enough to be alone on the open, clear plains. But the bush held even greater peril behind camp as it met the forest of the Rift Wall. Why had he not awakened Bogo? But it was too late to think of that.

Curved thorns of wait-a-bit bushes clawed at his shirt-sleeve. A dik-dik no more than twelve inches tall sped out of his path to the safety of deeper shadows.

"Suzie! Suzie! Come back!"

There was no answer. Jay kept on. Then, at last, he caught a glimpse of his cousin. She crept on hands and knees through some thick acacia thorn bushes.

"Suzie! Wait!"

Suzannah turned around. Her face was red as sunset and covered with scratches, tears, and dirt. "I can't find him, Jay! I thought he went in here. Then he disappeared like he'd made himself invisible."

Jay worked his way to her side. "I know. That's a zebra's color protection for you. Black and white stripes just mix with light and branches and . . . poof! . . . the zebra's gone. But we've got to be careful. There are rhinos in here. Heaps of them. Come on back to camp and we'll get Bogo to help us look."

Suzannah's eyes filled with tears. She stared around frantically. "But something'll catch Smudge."

"We're breaking strict rules being here!" argued Jay. "I could take care of myself, but you can't.   Come on back."

Suzannah glared at him with angry tears in her dark eyes.   "You're *scared,* Jay Clifford, that's all.   You're always looking down your nose at me because you think I'm such a sissy, and now you're the one who's scared!   Well, I'm not!   I'm going to find Smudge and you can just go back to camp and . . . and make your old elephant-hair bracelet."

Without waiting for an answer, Suzannah shoved past Jay and dashed ahead, following a narrow game trail.   She was quickly out of sight among the undergrowth.

Jay started after her, but the girl had a head start.   He could hear her plunging through the bushes like a frightened calf.   The animal trail divided.   Jay hesitated, trying to decide which way to go.   Then he started left, but had only gone a few steps when something caught him up short.

Something large and gray loomed beyond a dense growth of bushes. At first it looked like a rock. Then it moved jerkily. Jay caught his lower lip between his teeth, backing up a step. Rhino!

Luckily for Suzannah, she had either passed the animal downwind so that it missed her scent, or else she had gone by too quickly to disturb it. But as Jay backed against a tree, the rhino shifted nervously around, snuffling the air, aroused by an unwelcome smell of humans. The animal was not in a good mood.

Jay glimpsed part of the rhino's head through the tangle of branches. He saw a small round eye set in a dark, wrinkled face. A thick, curving horn. The eye would not see him unless he moved, for rhinos had poor eyesight. Just the same, it seemed to glare wickedly.

Suddenly the big animal moved, charging what it smelled. It crashed blindly through the bushes, tossing rocks and puffing with anger. Jay bolted aside and broke into a run.

The rhino quickly lost Jay's scent and plunged through trees well below him. Jay knew he was safe for the moment. He paused to catch his breath, and his knees ached from fright.

Still shaky, the boy hurried after Suzannah. He knew many tricks of tracking, and it wasn't hard to spot twigs that had been broken in a certain way, or to detect the faint mark left by a small shoe. He found Smudge's hoof prints, too.

Farther and farther, deeper and deeper into the dense

country, went the tracks. The rhino had delayed Jay too long! He and Suzannah were dangerously far from camp.

At last Jay found Suzannah. Hot and winded and trembling, she had stopped to rest on a rock. Tangled strands of hair clung to her tear-streaked cheeks, and with huge relief in her eyes she watched Jay coming.

"I . . . I saw him a minute ago," she blurted out. "Then he ran away from me. He acts as if it's another game. But I know he's close by. Please help find him, Jay. Please, *please!*"

Jay hesitated, then answered slowly. "Well . . . since we've come this far we'll go just a bit farther. I think I see where he went through here. But try not to make any noise. And let me lead. Don't even talk."

"Why not?" demanded Suzannah.

"So we can have a chance of spotting animals . . . or hearing them . . . before we're in trouble with them."

The forest opened around them. Thorn bushes disappeared. Vines and branches formed a ceiling above, while tiny flowers peeked from mats of creepers at their feet. As he and his cousin clambered over rocks crusted with moss and trudged across carpets of tiny-leafed plants, Jay began to forget his fears. The shadowy dry bush lay behind. The cool forest around them seemed peaceful and friendly.

Still, Jay knew it was unsafe for them to be there—just he and Suzannah alone. Anything could happen. And something soon did.

CHAPTER SEVEN

Mighty and the Mite

They found Smudge up to his shoulders in sun-dappled ferns. He had tired of hide-and-seek at last. The neat, pin-striped face gazed up at them innocently. Suzannah was upon him in moments, her scratched arms clutching the fuzzy shoulders. Smudge nuzzled her arm.

"I guess I'll have to carry him back or he'll run off again," sighed Jay. "Oh well, it's downhill going back."

Suzannah sank to the ground. "Jay, I'm so tired I can't move. Let's rest here, just for a minute."

Jay glanced into the trees around them. His breath caught as he heard a noise. Or had he imagined it? He stood up, holding his breath to listen, but the forest held its quiet. Then a different sound pierced the air. It was strong and vibrant and clear like a flute. It sounded from high above them on the forested mountainside.

"What was that?" Suzannah started. Her eyes grew wide.

"A bird," said Jay, smiling. "A golden oriole. It's an African kind, not like the ones you have at home." Jay forgot about danger. In his heart he thanked the oriole for choosing that moment to call, for its song was one of the most beautiful sounds of the African forest. Suzannah's face lit with a wondering smile.

As if it knew, the oriole called again from its faraway perch. Ringing, sweet, and clear came the sound. The forest seemed suddenly enchanted.

"Ooooh," breathed Suzannah. Hardly moving, still listening, she began to gaze at the trees with their mossy green trunks as if seeing them for the first time. She watched dust particles swirl and dance within golden shafts of sunlight. A barbet winged among the leaves for an instant, then vanished.

Jay began poking among the trees, looking for animal tracks or insects for his collection. He grinned as he spotted something on the ground and called Suzannah to see.

With Smudge clutched in her arms, Suzannah joined her cousin and bent to look. Hoof prints no longer than the tip of Suzannah's little finger made criss-cross patterns in the bare earth.

"So tiny," breathed Suzannah. "They must be tracks of a baby deer . . . but a most tiny, tiny baby deer."

Jay shook his head. "There aren't any real deer in Africa. These were made by a full-grown animal called a duiker. They look a bit like deer, really, but they're no taller than your knee. They've got wee little horns about as long as a kitchen match."

Suzannah eyed the hoof marks. "Well now. You don't say," she murmured. "Jay, do you suppose the tiny wee duiker is close by? Perhaps we could see it if we looked."

"Perhaps," answered Jay. He knew that the timid little antelope would have fled at the first sign of people. But he pretended for Suzannah's sake. She had never known the excitement of tracking a wild animal on foot.

"We'll follow," said Jay. "Maybe we'll have a glimpse of him. But be quiet. Quiet as you possibly can. Here, I'll carry Smudge and you just watch where you walk."

The baby zebra willingly let Jay carry him. His knobby long legs flopped limply against the boy's thighs with each step. Smudge was tired.

They picked their way downhill, toward camp. Jay stopped now and then, pretending to find fresh duiker tracks. The stops gave him time to listen carefully, to study the shadows around them. If only they could avoid another rhino! What was that noise?

After a few minutes of walking, Jay's sharp ears caught an unmistakable sound. Three times before, he had believed he heard it, then had been unsure. Now there could be no doubt.

The sound was a dull, odd rumbling. Jay knew well what it meant. Elephants! He held his breath to listen, and tried to judge the direction of the noise. He studied each tree and shadow and tangle of vines.

"What's the matter?" Suzannah had heard nothing, and her whisper was loud. "Do you see something?"

Jay winced and threw his cousin a sharp look that warned her to be silent. He dared not speak. He dared not make the smallest noise. But Suzannah didn't understand.

"Jay, something's wrong. I can tell! What is it?" She clutched the sleeve of his shirt and he could feel panic in her fingers. Jay knew she sensed his own fright. Suppose she should cry out, or run?

Jay thought fast. Then he forced himself to smile. "Why . . . nothing's wrong," he whispered softly. "It's just that I . . . I think we're close to the duiker. I don't want to scare it."

What a risky business to whisper like that! If the elephant were close enough, its sharp ears would catch the voices. They must get away quickly.

Jay wasted no more time. His eyes still searching ahead and to each side, he picked a silent path through the trees. Suzannah followed, and he knew she was trying to step softly. Now the forest was still. Now a bird called. A monkey skittered along a branch. Jay hurried.

Then a certain shadowy part of the forest ahead held his glance. Light through the overhead leafy tangle was spotty, so that the place was dim as a room with slatted shades. Shapes and shadows blended. But sensing something odd there, Jay slowed down and then stopped.

A dull "flump flump" greeted his listening senses. He knew it would be an elephant's huge ears, fanning out from its shoulders, then dropping back again. The noise was clearer than the rumbling, and helped the boy guess its direction. Smudge began to squirm restlessly. Jay clutched him tighter.

As Jay stared, shadows became shapes beyond some

trees. He sucked in his breath and held it. An elephant stood not more than fifteen yards away!

For a moment, Jay's mind whirled and he felt close to panic. He forced himself back to calm. Then, although his hands were clammy and his temples pounded, he felt a tingling excitement and a growing curiosity.

The huge animal did not know they were there. His

body was dappled with sun and shadows, blending with them well. Jay could pick out details only by staring until his eyes burned. He knew his cousin saw nothing yet, and he was glad of it. The elephant was dozing, as the big animals often did during the heat of the day. That was the reason Jay and Suzannah had been able to come so close without being noticed. The craggy skull rested gently against a tree trunk. Now, as if in a dream, the ears fanned out from the elephant's head like big wings. Then they dropped back.

Jay made out long curving tusks. At first he couldn't believe what he saw. He had thought their tips were out of sight among shadows. Then he saw one of them poking

beyond a low tree limb. Only one elephant had tusks that could span that distance!

Jay's lips moved, soundlessly forming the name as it burned across his mind. Mighty Mo.

At that moment the gray shape moved. The giant head no longer leaned against the tree. Noiselessly the elephant turned, and the full curve of his tusks came into the sun. The tip of his trunk began to trace small circles in the air. Then it lifted higher and higher, as if making question marks. He was searching for the scent of something that had disturbed his slumber. Perhaps the breeze had changed. Jay's pulse quickened.

Now Suzannah had seen Mighty Mo. She gave a small cry of terror and shrank back. "Jay . . . *look!*" Her warning came in a cry half-stifled with panic.

The sound of her voice brought Mighty Mo around in a quarter turn to face them head on. Now there could be no doubt. The elephant knew they were there. Jay turned, intending to make a dash. Then he remembered the *askari*. The mean one-tusker might be anywhere nearby. Perhaps Suzannah and he should stay still.

Suddenly restless, Smudge chose that one unlucky instant to wrench free from Jay's arms. Or perhaps he sensed Jay's uneasiness. Jay had no time to grab for him. Saucy ears, fuzz-ridged back, and neat striped hocks were gone among the bushes.

Mighty Mo had moved closer, into full view. His trunk was half raised and his ears were spread to catch sound.

82

Seconds ticked by as Jay hesitated.   Suzannah clutched his arm.

"Run!   Jay, let's run!"   Her voice was shrill.

"Stay still.   Don't move!" Jay hissed in return.

In the next moment, a strange thing happened.   Mohammed's ears fell back to his shoulders and his trunk lowered.   Something else held the elephant's attention.

It was Smudge.

The little zebra knew no fear.   Drawn by curiosity, he trotted directly toward the spot where the giant elephant stood.   He stopped once, stared up.   Then he broke into a

bold trot. He stopped again, now directly before Mighty Mo. His upturned muzzle just reached the elephant's knee.

Jay's mouth dropped open. He forgot about running away. He heard Suzannah gasp softly.

Mohammed the Mighty stepped backward to look down at the tiny creature that braved his power and temper. Then the sensitive tip of his trunk curled, and he touched the striped shoulder, the downy soft hairs along the neck, and the round bulge between Smudge's bright eyes. The trunk that could uproot trees became gentle as a feather.

Smudge seemed delighted. He wheeled about and gave the elephant an impish flick of his heels. Then with a sudden buck and a bound, he raced to one side, skidded, turned, and darted under Mohammed's belly. Just as if it were only a big bridge built for his play.

Mighty Mo whirled about. Though a glancing blow from one of his feet or his trunk could have ended Smudge forever, he placed his feet with the care of a nesting bird among her eggs. Mohammed was actually playing!

But the strange game soon ended. The elephant seemed disturbed once more by some sound, some smell in the air. Once more his long tusks raked the air as his trunk lifted. Again the ears fanned wide, and the span of them hid the trees beyond.

Jay's blood froze. Why had they waited so long? He grabbed Suzannah's arm. But at that moment, Mohammed turned away. His great padded feet made no sound. Like magic, he vanished into the trees behind him. He was gone.

As for Smudge, he glanced after his new friend as if bewildered. Then he stamped an angry little hoof. A moment later, and without a look backward, he trotted off in search of Mighty Mo.

"Smudge!" Suzannah called out despairingly.

Jay grabbed his cousin's hand. "Come on. We can't follow. We've got to get out of here."

Jay and Suzannah hardly paused until they reached the thick bushy growth near camp. Thirst tightened their throats. The heat of the parched dusty acacia country left their bodies dripping wet. Clothes torn, cheeks scratched and burning, they struggled on.

Soon they heard blasts from the horns of both Land-Rover and safari car. Voices called them. For the first time, Jay realized how worried everyone at camp would be. And relief flooded him like a bright big wave when he saw Bogo coming toward them through the bushes, with Big Charlie close behind.

Suzannah rushed toward the two scouts and fell against Bogo with tears of relief.

Only June Clifford remained in camp when the four of them arrived. Rob Clifford, long since returned from his own safari, had set out with Daniel to look for Jay and Suzannah. Two other scouts, newly arrived, were also combing the countryside. Tears of relief in her eyes, Jay's mother ran toward the boy and girl, while Bogo hurried to sound an "all safe" signal on the Land-Rover horn.

Soon afterward, June Clifford tended cuts and bruises as they sat around the table in the main tent. Willy poured glass after glass of cool water, then lemon soda. When Jay's father returned, he was so relieved to find the wanderers safe that he spared them the familiar lecture about leaving camp alone. That would surely come later. Now he listened to the story of the afternoon and asked questions.

The scouts crowded into the tent to hear. Bogo and Big Charlie, their faces serious and quiet. Killi, the Masai tracker who had come that afternoon to join them. Another new scout, Saidi, looked incredulous. The Wanderobo, Daniel, kept his usual silence.

Suzannah slowly recovered from her fright, and her voice choked with tears as she began to miss Smudge. "Will I ever see him again?"

Nobody answered right away. Then June Clifford spoke gently as she replaced iodine and adhesive patches in the first-aid box. "We may find him again. None of us will give up hope yet."

Ranger Clifford leaned across the camp table. "I've got a full team of scouts now, Suzie. One of them brought some news from the village that may change things."

Jay had been toying halfheartedly with one of the elephant-hair bracelets. He looked up quickly. His father's voice had an especially grave note.

"There has been an elephant raid on the *shambas*," said the ranger. "It was last night. Two elephants were seen. There was no doubt they were Mighty Mo and his *askari*. A man was badly hurt. Crops were damaged."

Jay moaned. "That . . . means you've got to . . . to . . . ."

Suzannah finished the thought. "You've got to shoot Mighty Mo?"

The ranger pressed his lips together, frowning in a troubled way. Then he shook his head. "Perhaps not. There's a good part to all this mess. The farmers seem to agree that all the damage was done by the little one-tusk elephant. Certainly, he was the one who charged the man. They say the big elephant behaved oddly, just stayed his distance and watched."

"But Mighty Mo was with him," said Mrs. Clifford unhappily. "That sides him with the troublemaker."

"What are you going to do?" asked Jay.

"Look for them.   Tomorrow."

"What if you find them?" queried Suzannah.

"I don't exactly know and that's the truth of it," answered Rob Clifford.   "I don't want to see the big fellow go down, but he's in bad company.   Maybe he's got the makings of a rogue himself.   Anyway, Suzannah, we'll have a look about for Smudge."

By late afternoon, a blue rainstorm moved like a veil across the horizon above the lake.   The fever trees behind camp turned green-gold like the grasses, and the low light of a sinking sun struck the backs of a zebra herd.   Then the sky turned apricot and turquoise, and the bush country grayed into shadows.

Jay scrubbed for dinner.   He wandered a few yards out on the plains, feeling the restlessness of coming dark and coming rain.   His mind was filled with thoughts of the big elephant.

CHAPTER EIGHT

No *Returning*

During the night, clouds covered all the stars. The first big drop of rain plopped against a leaf. Soon, Jay awakened to hear rain pounding against the tent roof. Dismal thoughts of Smudge and Mighty Mo kept him sleepless beneath his mosquito netting. Their tracks would be washed away behind them. How could anyone find them?

He slapped at a mosquito that had found its way under the netting. Then he heard his father's voice from the cot across the tent. The ranger, too, had been lying awake. "Rainy season may come early this year," he said.

"Umm." Jay turned over in the darkness and lifted himself up on one elbow. "Dad, I've been thinking more and more about the big tusker . . . Mighty Mo. I'm sure he's the same elephant, Mohammed, that Suli talked about."

"After thirty years? Still, it's possible. I guess we'll never know."

Jay didn't say anything more for a while. Then he

spoke almost hesitantly. "Dad . . . I've wondered if I could shoot an elephant myself. I mean . . . if I had to do it."

There was a long pause in the darkness. The rain pounded steadily against the canvas. Then Jay's father answered slowly. "Perhaps you could do it. You've got a good eye and a steady arm. And you've practiced. Your day will come. I warn you, though. Your heart may be heavier than you dream . . . after it's done."

By morning the grasslands were awash, and the rain still drove down. It blotted out the grasslands and hid the highlands behind camp. Nonetheless, Rob Clifford, Bogo, and two other scouts started out on foot. They had promised to try. Try they would. Daniel stayed behind to guard camp.

"They won't be able to see a thing in all this rain," Suzannah said sadly. She sat in the main tent, chin in her hands. "I think they're brave to go at all."

"Oh, the rain's nothing to them. Just means they won't get so hot walking," Jay answered lightly.

At noon the rain suddenly stopped. Jay and Suzannah heard last thunder rolls in the distance. A strip of sky threw aside its gray shield to show a pale blue. A crested crane strutted through a mud puddle near the tents, shaking its damp golden crown.

Late that afternoon, June Clifford paced restlessly back and forth in the main tent. Suddenly she stopped and turned to Daniel. The scout was checking the barrel of his gun.

"Daniel, do you think the safari car would get stuck on the plains? Is the mud too bad? I thought we might take a turn toward the south. Maybe we'd meet the others and save them some walking back. It would save us all this sitting and wondering and fretting."

Daniel looked doubtful. "Lorry might make it, *memsahib*," he said. "Then again . . . mud is bad."

"Let's try anyway!" exclaimed Jay, hopping to his feet. They decided to go.

A late afternoon sun burned warmly by the time the safari car started away. Puddles still made mirrors in the grass. Sometimes the tires skidded and spun in mud that looked like thick black grease. But they kept on going, trying to avoid the worst spots.

They reached a spot six miles from camp. Before them, tangled acacia thorn bushes looked gray and forbidding. There had been no sign of the ranger and his scouts. Mrs. Clifford eyed the sinking sun and sighed, "We'd best turn back."

Suzannah was watching five ostriches running across the plains behind them, swaying slightly, plumes puffed. Daniel stopped the safari car as they watched.

"They look as if they had ballet-dancer costumes on," said Suzannah. "All those plumes."

Daniel started the engine and the safari car lurched ahead. Without warning, the tires began to slip in mud. Daniel pushed harder on the gas pedal. The rear wheels fought the mud, but sank deeper. Then deeper and deeper. Jay's mother bit her lip anxiously.

Jay hopped to the ground, eyeing the thick black mud under the truck. "Hold on, Daniel. We're in a hole."

Sure enough, the first slipping of the wheels had dropped one rear tire into a pothole. Whirling through the greasy stuff had mired the safari car firmly. Mrs. Clifford slipped behind the driver's wheel while Jay and Daniel pushed from behind. Even Suzannah tried to help, not heeding the mud that sprayed her face and clothes. It was no use.

"Well, we can get out the jack," suggested Jay. "We can lift the rear end with it and push the car clear."

His mother shook her head. "We broke the jack last month, remember? It's still being repaired."

Nobody spoke for a few moments. They watched the stranded lorry as if hoping that their hard stares would cause it to suddenly heave itself free. Then Suzannah, her face mud-spattered, asked the hardest question. "What are we going to do?"

"I suppose we could walk back to camp from here. It's about six miles," suggested Jay.

June Clifford sat calmly on the front seat of the safari car and shook her head. "No. We haven't enough daylight and we brought no torches. If it should rain hard again . . . well, you know this country. Water from that mountain will pour down on us and we'll be caught in a flash flood. No sir! We stay right where we are."

Suzannah's eyes were round and thoughtful. She nodded wisely. "At night, all the rhinos and buffaloes come out to graze. They'll be right out on the plains, won't they?"

"We're safer in the truck," said Jay's mother. "By morning the ground will be dry enough to move."

Afternoon became a gold and scarlet sunset. A herd of "tommy" gazelles wandered closer than usual and stopped to look at them. A baby gazelle, days old, bounded behind its mother. Now and then it would spring straight up in the air, tiny legs stiff as sticks, tassel tail switching.

Sunset dropped away before a shadowy dusk, and the stars came out.

"It's beautiful and scary . . . both at the same time," Suzannah commented. A bush-baby howled mournfully from a tree.

"That's our part of Africa, start to finish," said Mrs. Clifford, resting her head back on the car seat. She was watching the stars and the acacia trees. "I hate to think all of this may some day be farms. No more giraffes. No more lions being scary at night."

"You like it even when it's scary, don't you, Aunt June?" asked Suzannah. "And so does Jay."

"I guess we're crazy, but we do, Suzie," answered Mrs. Clifford softly. Then she straightened suddenly and clapped her hands. "I just remembered something! There's a whole box of biscuits under the seat, all wrapped in cellophane and fresh and unopened. We won't starve, not us!" She rummaged quickly beneath the seat and with a flourish brought out a tin box.

"Hooray for Mum!" cried Jay. "Daniel, let's find some of those roots you like to eat. Quick, before it's too dark. Then we can build a fire and roast them."

Daniel's face stretched in a grin. "*N'dio*. And I think I can find clean rain water to drink."

Soon, Jay and Daniel worked over a fire. A heap of brownish round roots lay beside it. The rain-soaked wood sputtered at first, so they used bits of dry paper and a broken crate from the safari car. Tiny flames gathered heat and the wet wood caught, twig by twig. At last the fire glowed red and strong, and a handful of roots were roasting. Later, they sat on the seat of the safari car, staring into the flames and hungrily munching biscuits and sweet roots.

Never had the stars seemed so brilliant and large. In the distance they could hear a lion's grunt. Jay gave Suzannah an encouraging smile. "That just means he's already found his supper. He'll just stay where he is and snarl at all his friends."

The fire threw a bright glow on Suzannah's face. "I hope . . . I hope his supper isn't . . . isn't Smudge." She swallowed the last of a biscuit, half choking on it.

After a while, Suzannah and Jay's mother stretched out on two seats of the safari car, leaving the empty rear for Daniel and Jay. The Wanderobo scout threw more wood on the fire, then stared into the night.

Jay liked Daniel almost better than Bogo. Daniel had a secret way about him, but he was wise. Jay decided it was because he had lived among animals for so long. He always knew more than he would tell, unless people pressed him to talk.

"Are you listening to something, Daniel?" Jay asked, watching the firelight play on the bony planes of the scout's face. "What do you hear?"

"It is not exactly what I hear," murmured Daniel. "It is something I feel."

96

"What?"

"Elephants," said Daniel with calm. "There are elephants near."

Jay felt a shiver through his body. "I don't expect they'll bother us," he said.

"No, they will not bother us."

Later Jay asked a question that had weighed heavily on his mind. "Daniel, do you think Mighty Mo ought to be killed?"

"No," answered the scout simply.

"How about the *askari?*"

Daniel shrugged. "I don't like to see any elephant shot. Once Africa was the wild animal's country. It was not man's country. It is wrong for men to kill so many animals. Some day there will be none left."

Daniel paused.

"Still," he went on, "this elephant has done wrong against man. I suppose he must die for it."

CHAPTER NINE

The Lion

At last, Jay slept deeply on the floor of the safari car. The brilliant stars drifted westward, then dimmed with the coming dawn. He awakened when a shaft of sunlight glanced through the front windshield, and glowed warmly on his suntanned arm. Daniel opened his eyes, yawning. Suzannah and Mrs. Clifford still slept.

Quietly, Jay undid the large snaps that held the rear canvas flaps in place. He squeezed out. How good to feel the sun! Jay tossed his arms back and forth to chase a cramp. It had been hard, that metal floor! A dryness in his throat made him remember the rushing stream at Mto-Wa-Mbu. Then he thought longingly of one of Willy's big breakfasts.

Daniel dropped to hands and knees by the rear wheels of the safari car. He poked at the drying mud. "Eh, good. We will soon free this foolish thing."

Jay glanced about. Shadows still dwelled in the forests of the mountain wall behind them. But the eastern sky above the soda lake glowed apricot and gold and blue. Sun streamed upward and across the plains.

Jay's feet had a will of their own. Leaving Daniel to worry about mud beneath the wheels, he skirted thickets. A brownish duiker no taller than his knee popped from the shadows, then vanished. At his feet, Jay saw a scarab beetle patiently pushing a dusty wad of dung three times its size.

"Jay?"

It was Suzannah. She was stumbling through the thickets behind him, shading her eyes against the sun. Jay stopped to wait until she caught up.

"Where are you going?"

"Nowhere special. Just looking about. Come along."

Suzannah seemed eager to join him. She fell into step. "Daniel says to be careful. He says there are elephants around. We're not to go far."

"Oh, Daniel said that last night, too." Jay shrugged carelessly. Just the same, he looked around with extra caution.

Walking grew harder. The countryside here was broken by dry angular shapes of scrub acacias. Their shirts caught on thorns of wait-a-bit bushes. Glancing back, Jay noticed that the safari car was out of sight.

A few minutes later, they stopped to look at a pair of Bat-eared foxes nestled side by side in their hole. Fuzzy oversized ears showed darkly through the tawny grasses.

Two pairs of brilliant black eyes glared defiantly at the intruders. Jay grinned delightedly. Then he felt Suzannah tug sharply at his sleeve.

"Jay! Look! Please look over there!"

At first, Jay was annoyed. Suzannah's voice had frightened the two little animals. But as he turned, he saw real alarm in his cousin's eyes. "I'm sure I see a . . . a big animal," said Suzannah.

Jay's eyes followed his cousin's pointing finger. Beyond some low bushes, he saw a rough, sunny clearing. Green-trunked fever trees made a lazy canopy over shadowy bush country beyond. Then Jay saw a long yellowish shape among the grasses, just matching them. His heart jumped. It was a lion!

The big cat lay low, its belly flat to the ground. It did not see them. It eyed something beyond the clearing. The lion was only half-grown. Hardly more than a year old, Jay judged. As yet no mane pushed from its tawny neck. The large paw that curled against the earth belonged to an awkward youngster.

Should they run? The open grasslands stretched behind. Or stay still? Perhaps they would be safe if they remained quietly hidden.

Only yards away, thickly tangled branches of some thornscrub made a protected place. Tapping Suzannah's arm, Jay motioned toward them. They crawled to the spot. Quiet as wary antelopes, they peered through thorns and tiny leaves.

100

Jay had watched many lions. He could tell that the half-grown cat aquiver with excitement, hadn't learned all the rules of hunting. An experienced lion could lie still as a stone near its prey, slipping forward by sudden moves that were almost too quick for the eye.

"Just a cub," Jay whispered close to Suzannah's ear. He tried to make his tone reassuring. "Not even smart enough to know we're here."

"What's he doing?" asked Suzannah in a tremulous whisper.

"Stalking."

A moment later, Jay saw something move at the far side of the clearing. An animal's hindquarters, small hindquarters, broke a pattern of yellow-green branches. Suzannah saw it too. She started. Then Jay could hear his cousin moan.

It was Smudge.

Dismayed, Jay watched the little zebra step unknowingly into the open, heading for a puddle of water. It glistened invitingly in the sunlight. Moments later, Smudge was bending over the puddle, legs braced apart. He drank thirstily, blinking with each welcome gulp. Jay thought how hungry Smudge must be. Then he wondered how the little zebra had survived for a day and two nights without being caught by other lions or by other enemies. There could be only one answer. It made him feel shivery to think of it. Smudge might still be with Mighty Mo!

The lion inched toward Smudge, wriggling like a fish. Its chin was low to the ground, its round ears flat against its head. At any moment it would spring. Jay thought of throwing a stone to scare the big cat. But it might turn on them. Jay knew he could take care of himself. He could yell, toss stones, then run like a cheetah. But he dared not take chances with Suzannah. She couldn't run fast. She might trip. She might be frozen with fright and be unable to move at all.

102

Even now Suzannah had both fists against her mouth, trying to keep herself from crying out.

Then Jay saw the third intruder in the clearing. At first he thought his eyes had tricked him. How could an elephant take shape from trees and shadows so suddenly? First nothing. Then the fever trees seemed to part and the huge animal loomed beyond Smudge like a living mountain.

Mighty Mo's ears spread rigidly, hiding the yellow-green and shadowy trees behind. He looked straight toward the young lion. A wild rage blazed in his eyes.

Still the cat kept his gaze on Smudge. He did not see the elephant because each sense had focused on his prey. He chose the next moment to spring.

Mighty Mo's trunk lifted high. A mighty trumpeting split the morning air. Smudge's striped head jerked up, spraying droplets of water into the sunlight. The startled lion twisted and veered in mid-air, but the elephant's furious challenge had spoiled his chances. Unsheathed claws bit bare earth, missing their mark while Smudge dashed to safety.

Again Mighty Mo screamed. Now he was charging! He shuffled toward the unlucky lion with the speed of a truck. First his trunk was raised, and Jay could see the wedge shape of his open mouth, the deep pink of its lining. Then the trunk curled under. Ivory saber tusks cut through grasses, bushes.

At first, Jay thought the lion had been trampled. But a quick twist of the cat's lithe body had saved it. Snarling

103

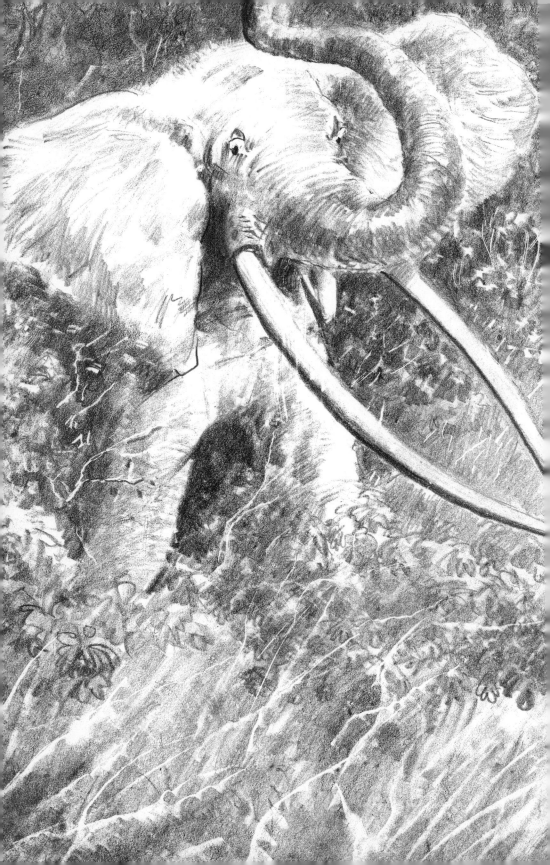

and confused, it rolled aside. Its jaws parted, showing per-
fect white fangs. It looked up over its shoulder, snarling
again. Then with a quick wrench to one side, it escaped
into the grasses.

Mighty Mo turned to watch the lion retreat. The big
elephant's tail waved. Jay could see the black bristles of
its tip. The elephant's head was tilted back, ears flared.
Again a mighty trumpeting, brassy, long, ear-splitting.

Hardly had the ringing settled in Jay's ears when he
felt Suzannah tug his sleeve. "Look. Bogo!" she said
breathlessly. "And Uncle Rob and Daniel!"

Jay's head whirled around. He saw relief chasing the
terror from Suzannah's eyes. Then he focused on the shadowy trees beyond. There, crouching motionless, were
Daniel and his father. The ranger must have found the
safari car on his way back to camp.

Bogo had crept within yards of Jay and Suzannah.
He moved with care, speed, and silence. His rifle was
clutched close to his chest. Now he stood above them. His
strong arms swooped down to scoop up Suzannah. In almost the same swift move, he tossed the gun to Jay.

"You carry this," Bogo hissed. "Carry gun while I
carry Suzannah. Follow. Quick before the elephant turns
this way again."

Bogo's chin motioned Jay to follow. He was already
ducking beneath branches, around bushes. There was no
time to spare.

But Jay did not move. The gun rested heavily on his arms, the barrel cool to the clutch of his left fist. The stock lay solid and hard against his chest. Still kneeling, Jay twisted toward the clearing. In a moment he would follow Bogo. In a moment . . . .

But just as Jay turned, Mighty Mo turned. He shifted his giant weight without hurry. Those ears still flared like weathered, storm-tossed sails. Those eyes, still wild and angry. The curved tips of ivory tusks hovered a foot above yellowed grasses.

Jay started to slip away. Then he hesitated.

Mighty Mo stared unwaveringly, straight at Jay. Behind the gray giant rose a wall of trees. But between the elephant and the kneeling boy lay only one frail bush and a grassy clearing of about fifteen yards.

CHAPTER TEN

When You Face an Elephant

A silence rose from the drying twigs and grasses around Jay. The silence hovered in the trees beyond the clearing. The absolute stillness of sky, forest, and bush made a drumming of Jay's heartbeat.

The ranger's son knew much about elephants. He knew from watching them, and he knew from the talk he had heard for years, ever since he had been able to understand. An elephant would stand watching and waiting. No warning came before a charge. The ears might flare. Then the peace would be broken by an attack so sudden, rapid, and exploding with sound that only the coolest-headed men could save themselves.

No time now to look for help from his father or the scouts. They would know that noise and motion might cause Mighty Mo to charge. Perhaps he had no choice but to stay motionless.

Suddenly the thoughts racing through Jay's mind were

not thoughts of running away. Had he not wondered for years what he would do, face to face with an angry elephant? "You will meet the test of an elephant hunt," Oriono had said. The words burned deep.

Something calm and ungiving settled inside Jay Clifford. His arms felt strong around the heavy gunstock. What steadiness in them as he lifted the gun to his shoulder to aim at the correct spot on the elephant's sloping skull. Bogo's rifle wasn't a full-size elephant gun. It was only a medium-bore rifle. That meant Jay must not miss his mark, not by the smallest fraction of an inch! Still, how often he had practiced! If Mohammed meant to charge, let Mohammed come!

The ears flared more rigidly. Now they were not like old gray sails. Now they were taut banners. Jay jammed the stock harder into his shoulder. He knew how that gun kicked back when it fired.

A second passed. Two. Three seconds. Mighty Mo seemed to tower above Jay in the clearing. Yet more than that, the giant elephant seemed a part of the shadowy trees just beyond him. Part of the earth beneath his gray post legs, too. He was solid as the earth, strong and rough as the earth. And like the earth, both secret and alive.

All of a sudden, Jay felt like an intruder in the world of Mighty Mohammed. The giant elephant had a look of patience and waiting rather than a look of fury.

Jay let the gun barrel drop slightly. The long curved

tusks were as ivory scepters of a forest king. Daniel's words came to Jay like an echo. This was the wild animal's land, not man's. And Suli's words. The elephant came in peace.

Jay heard his own voice whispering, "Go away, Mighty Mo."

For perhaps three more seconds the giant elephant watched. The ears had drifted back, furling against gray shoulders. The tip of his trunk curled out, then under. Sun made shadows above green-black eyes that had seen more than half a century of life.

Jay stood straight, the gun an idle weight in his hands. Mighty Mo had already turned on giant padded feet. With no sound, he vanished into the trees.

Jay whispered in Swahili, *"Kwa heri."* It meant "farewell."

CHAPTER ELEVEN

The Askari's Last Charge

Jay watched, as if held by a spell, while the trees and shadows closed behind Mighty Mo. He didn't see Smudge at first. The baby zebra had wandered back into the clearing. His dainty hoofs rested on the very spot where Mighty Mo had stood watching Jay. Smudge looked tired and lost.

Jay hardly noticed until Suzannah suddenly bolted from the trees, off to Jay's right. She headed straight for Smudge. Jay heard voices. First his father shouted. Then Bogo. Then his mother's shriek of warning.

"Suzannah! Come back!"

"Look OUT! The *askari!*"

"Come back! COME BACK!"

The silence broke into sound that seemed to come from all sides at once. From behind and to the left came a shrill trumpeting. It was not Mighty Mo. The din was tinny and blustering. Branches cracked and a tree slammed earthward.

Jay looked around, wild-eyed. Then his blood froze. Hardly twenty feet from Suzannah, the *askari* shuffled forward. With deadly speed he moved toward Suzannah and Smudge, trunk curled under, eyes glinting.

Hardly thinking, Jay whipped into action. He jammed the gunstock against his shoulder. His grip tightened. He aimed.

CR . . . *AAK!!*

The *askari* stopped as if he had slammed into a wall. Jay saw a shudder travel through the big body. He saw the look of defiance draining from the elephant's eyes.

Then the *askari* dropped in his tracks.

Later, as they walked back to the safari car, Jay felt his father's strong fingers press into his shoulder. The boy was grateful for the quiet, steadying grip. He felt shaky and dazed. His ears were ringing. As if from far away he heard the familiar calls of birds, twigs snapping, a new squeak in one of Bogo's shoes.

Bogo walked ahead, carrying Smudge. June Clifford kept close to Suzannah, one arm around the girl's shoulder. Suzannah had been badly frightened, but she had been too stubbornly brave to cry.

Jay's father had been the first to reach his side after the *askari* fell. He had gently taken the gun from Jay's hands. The ranger hadn't been able to speak at first.

113

Then he kept repeating the same words, over and over, in a hoarse sort of voice. "Good work. That was a tough go. Good work. Good work, Jay."

With many hands pushing, the wheels of the safari car lurched out of the hole. Soon they were bumping toward camp. The paleness left Suzannah's lips, and her eyes lost their look of fright. Gradually, the shaky group of people began to talk about all that had happened.

"Big Charlie saw your campfires last night. We'd decided to stay where we were until morning. Of course we didn't know the fire was yours. We came to check this morning."

"Daniel had left to look for Jay and Susie," said Mrs. Clifford. "He left his gun with me because he wasn't really worried. Of course I forgot it. That's why we had only one among us . . . Bogo's . . . when the trouble started."

Before long they were gathered around the table in the camp's main tent. Willy heaped helping after helping of

meat and eggs, fruit, cheese, and bread on big plates. Suzannah fed Smudge two bottles of milk from his soda bottle.
Soon his sides were full to popping, like a striped balloon.

"You ought to be grateful to Mighty Mo!" Suzannah
scolded, wagging a finger at Smudge. You should *indeed*
be grateful . . . just as I'm grateful to Jay."

"I'm sorry I had to shoot poor old one-tusk," Jay said,
staring down at his plate. "Mean as he was."

"I guess it was all my fault," murmured Suzannah
sadly. "Because I ran out in the clearing after Smudge.
I'm sorry."

"You couldn't have known about the *askari,* Suzie,"
Rob Clifford said in a level voice. "As for Jay, he did a
man's job, and did it well. But I'm just as proud of a decision he made before that . . . when he put down his gun
and let Mighty Mo go his way."

Jay looked up in surprise. His father understood that!
Truly, he understood!

Daniel spoke. "The ranger's son waited like a man.
He did not shoot hastily, as a thoughtless young one might
have done. It was brave."

Jay jabbed his fork into scrambled eggs that he knew
he would not taste. He shivered, remembering how close
he had been to squeezing that trigger.

At that moment, Willy hurried through the rear of the
tent. "*Bwana,* two runners have come from the village!"

Willy ducked aside to admit two African farmers.
116

One was tall, with ragged trousers cut short above his knees. The other was short and wore a battered felt hat with an ostrich feather.

"What is it? Come in." Rob Clifford strode across the tent to greet the newcomers.

"*Bwana!* It is the elephants again!" announced the farmer with ragged trousers.

"They came last night," said the short one. "Crops were trampled again. Many crops."

Jay listened in stunned silence. His father had urged the two breathless runners to sit and rest. The ranger straddled his own chair, folding his arms across its back. "During the night, you say. Was anyone able to see what the elephants looked like in the dark?"

The two Africans nodded their heads hard. "*N'dio, Bwana.* We gathered more than fifty men with torches. We made noises to scare them. We saw the great elephant with tusks three arms long."

Jay felt his heart sinking.

"And the little one," added the tall farmer. "Eh, *Bwana,* he is the rogue. He almost killed two people."

"How about the big one?" Jay jumped to his feet.

"The big one? Eh, that was strange to see. The big one only watched. It was just like the other time. We think he only followed."

The farmer with the ostrich-feather hat grew excited. "If you would hunt the small one, *Bwana,* the farmers would be content. We could feel safe. We don't think the big one means evil."

Jay saw his father's shoulders lift—then fall, in a breath of relief. He slapped his knees and stood up. "In that case, your troubles are already over. The little one-tusker is dead. He was shot this morning."

The farmers' eyes grew wide. Then the tall one said, "We are glad, *Bwana*. We are grateful to you."

"You may thank my son," said Ranger Clifford, nodding toward Jay. "He brought down the little elephant with a single shot not two hours ago."

The ranger strode across the tent to find a jug of drinking water. Pouring two glasses for the hot and tired runners, he went on talking. "We're breaking camp this morning. I'll have to get back to file reports and so forth. We'll take you along. It will save you a long walk."

But the two Africans hardly seemed to be listening. They were staring at Jay in wide-eyed wonder. "You should be proud to have such a boy," said the tall one softly.

Jay listened no more. Hurrying from the tent, he stared toward the sun-dazzled grasslands until his eyes burned. But the burning came from sudden tears, not sun. Proud to have killed the *askari?* Jay was remembering the look in the elephant's eyes as it fell to earth. No, he was not proud.

Then Jay turned to face the green rise of the forest wall behind camp. His chest swelled. Somewhere in that

118

secret maze of trees, dampness, vines, and shadows, Mighty Mo would be ripping bark from a tree. Jay could almost hear the sound of it, smell the pungence of wood beneath, hear the flap of elephant ears.

Jay smiled now. People would talk of the *askari,* and of the boy who had shot him. Let them. But he, Jay, would be prouder of another moment. He had let a gun slip from his shoulder to spare an elephant.

CHAPTER TWELVE

Homeward Safari

Work began soon after breakfast. Cots were folded and lashed together. One by one, taut tent roofs crumpled into limp heaps on the ground. At last, camp by Lake Manyara remained only as yellowed patches of grass where each tent had stood.

Jay found Suzannah sitting beneath the big baobab tree, Smudge nearby.

"Look, Jay," Suzannah said, pointing. "Smudge is nuzzling grass as if he wanted to start grazing."

Jay smiled to see the soft nostrils flaring as Smudge blew the tough grasses. "He'll grow fast from now on."

Suddenly Suzannah looked sad. "How I shall miss him when Mother and Daddy take me back to London."

"You needn't, you know," said Jay. "He's yours, Suzie. If you want, Dad can arrange to send Smudge on to England for you. He'd have to stay in quarantine for a

while. And I guess he'd have to live in the zoo in London. But at least you'd have him near."

Suzannah shook her head, looking at him squarely. Her voice was full of determination. "I've thought it all over. You must keep him and raise him for me, Jay. You must raise him *wild*. He belongs wild."

Jay cocked his head in a puzzled way. "Wild? How?"

"I mean wild like other zebras. He must join a herd of zebras just as soon as he's old enough to take care of himself. He doesn't belong with people."

Jay started to argue. But he knew Suzannah was right. He admired her decision. "I'll do it," he said. "And I'll write you lots of letters to tell you how he gets along. Why, he'll probably take up with a herd right here near Lake Manyara."

Suzannah clapped her hands. "And I'll come back again and see him . . . all grown!"

Jay nodded, smiling.

Late that afternoon, the jeep and safari car were parked beneath the fig tree near the porch of the *duka*. Mud still stuck to the fenders, caked and gray. The Land-Rover had started to boil over after the hot trip.

The *duka* buzzed with people. Farmers in khaki shorts milled around the ramshackle porch. A goat bleated. Chickens and dogs and children chased about the dusty road in front of the store.

122

"Coming in, Jay?" asked Rob Clifford, hopping to the ground. "I've got some business with Sam, and I want to talk to some of the farmers about this elephant business."

Jay nodded. He jabbed at his shirt-tail to bury it more neatly beneath his belt. He followed the ranger and Bogo

into the cool, half-dark store. Sam, his blue turban wound high on his head, leaned across the counter. He stretched out a big hand in greeting.

A group of African farmers pressed close. News had spread quickly. All had heard what the game ranger's son had done. But the story had to be told again. Jay felt many eyes upon him, full of surprise and admiration. It seemed an endless time before he could break free.

Jay stepped out into the brilliant sunlight once more. In front of the porch, an excited cluster of farmers, women, and children had gathered in a circle. In the middle, Suzannah sat cross-legged in all the dust and dirt, grinning and giggling. More than a dozen African children were making friends with Smudge. The little zebra tripped from one delighted child to another, shoving his black muzzle against shoulders, grabbing shirtsleeves, and tossing his head. Suzannah was the color of the dust itself.

Jay's mother stood in the shade of the fig tree, her head tilted back with laughter. She called out to Jay, "Tell me, is that your cousin? I left here about ten days ago with a little niece from London, but this can't be the same child."

Jay grinned. He shoved his hands into his pockets. Then he heard a noise from the other side of the porch.

Bump. Bumpety-bump.

The treadle of the ancient sewing machine moved up and down, up and down. Jay turned. Suli bent over his
124

work, the violet turban slipping down over his tangled eyebrows.

For just a moment, Suli looked up. There was a pleased twinkle in his ancient eyes as he gazed at Jay. The Indian bent back over his sewing machine to hide a smile.

Bump . . . bumpety-bump went the treadle.

ABOUT THE AUTHOR AND ARTIST

JOCELYN ARUNDEL was born in Washington, D.C., and is a graduate of the National Cathedral School for Girls and Smith College. She also spent a summer at McGill University, studying French intensively in preparation for her junior year at the Sorbonne. After graduation she returned to Washington as a copy writer for the Washington Daily News and later went to Brussels to work with the International Union for Conservation. She has also been associated with the National Geographic Society in Washington, D.C. She is married and lives there now, with her husband and baby daughter, except for trips to her family's home in the Bahamas. The author of JINGO: WILD HORSE OF ABACO, and DUGAN AND THE HOBO, Jocelyn Arundel's first story SIMBA OF THE WHITE MANE resulted from a three-month safari in East Africa. The author's experiences in this safari also inspired MIGHTY MO.

WESLEY DENNIS has also been on safari in Africa, filling his sketchbook with its sights. He was born in Boston, Massachusetts, and began his art career while working for several Boston newspapers. He is well known throughout the children's book world and has illustrated many books, including Jocelyn Arundel's SIMBA OF THE WHITE MANE, JINGO: WILD HORSE OF ABACO, and DUGAN AND THE HOBO; Marguerite Henry's famous Newbery Award winner, KING OF THE WIND; Mildred Pace's OLD BONES, THE WONDER HORSE; Henry Larom's BRONCO CHARLIE and RIDE LIKE AN INDIAN! Mr. Dennis is author-artist of the famous *Flip* stories and A CROW I KNOW. He lives in Warrenton, Virginia.